D0021548

Sweet Reason

Sweet Reason

Sandy Steen

Five Star
Unity, Maine

Five Star Romance.
Published in conjunction with Writer's House, Inc.

Cover photograph by Nivette Jackaway

January 1998
Standard Print Hardcover Edition.

Five Star Standard Print Romance Series.

The text of this edition is unabridged.

Set in 11 pt. Plantin by Al Chase.

Printed in the United States on permanent paper.

Library of Congress Cataloging in Publication Data

Steen, Sandy.
   Sweet reason / Sandy Steen.
    p. cm.
   ISBN 0-7862-1259-4 (hc : alk. paper)
   I. Title.
  [PS3569.T3386S95   1998]
   813'.54—dc21   97-31796

For June Harvey
who showed me instead of telling me
how to make dreams come true.

Prologue

Caressive fingers wrapped around the butt of the unorthodox pistol. The metal grip nestled intimately into the well of his hand. Donald Barlow's stoic expression belied an unexpected loin-tightening sensation as his lean thumb stroked the side of the barrel. With practiced ease he hefted the gun from palm to palm, checking the weight and balance, savoring the feel of the weapon.

"How many can you get and how much will it cost me?"

"I can probably get you two, for say . . . half a mil."

Barlow narrowed his eyes, cutting the would-be seller with an icy look intended to threaten. It succeeded. The man began to sweat profusely in the cool Texas night.

"Watch it, Miller, or you'll price yourself right out of the market," Barlow warned.

"You don't scare me. I *am* the market. You can't go anywhere else and get this kind of equipment and we both know it."

Kyle Miller was a coward; the false bravado didn't fool Barlow for a minute and he pressed his advantage. "And we both know I could probably find another Reese employee just as enterprising, and perhaps a lot less greedy."

"Not while I'm around," the other man said, attempting a cocky grin.

"That can be arranged."

Miller swallowed the golf-ball-sized knot that suddenly obstructed his breathing.

"Now, suppose we cut the crap and get down to business," Barlow directed. "And this time, give me a reasonable quote."

"I, uh, guess maybe I could get you three for that price."

"Six."

"Just a damn minute." Once again Miller was fixed with the cold and lethal stare. "That's highway rob—"

"Four. My final offer. Take it or leave it."

Avarice momentarily forced Miller's self-protective instincts into second place. "Why, you bastard, you'll turn around and sell 'em to some commie country for three times what you're offering me. You low-life, son-of-a-bi—"

The word, choked off by stubby but powerful fingers, never made it past Miller's throat.

"You believe in living dangerously, don't you, friend." Barlow's hot breath hissed across the other man's mottled face. "Do yourself a favor: take the money and shut up." A look of pure loathing etched Barlow's face before he released his victim and took a step back.

Immediately, Miller's trembling fingers flew to assess the damage. Swallowing convulsively, his Adam's apple bobbed up and down as if he were making sure it still functioned. Carefully he backed around the hood of the truck until a distance of several feet separated the two men.

"Are you in a reasonable frame of mind now?"

Miller nodded, rubbing his neck.

"Here's the deal. Four guns for half a million, cash on delivery. All you have to do is furnish the merchandise. I take care of everything else, agreed?"

"Four is a lot. But . . . but I can . . . can probably do it," Miller hastened to add.

"Probably?"

"I can. It'll just take longer. Four will be harder to cover."

"When can you deliver?"

"Thirty, maybe forty-five days?"

"Done." Barlow placed the laser gun on top of the cassette-size power pack and handed them to his cohort. "Oh, and Miller, don't contact me again. I'll call you in thirty days. Understood?"

"Fine," Miller grunted as he slipped farther around to the driver's side of the Bronco. Jerking open the door, he slung himself into the front seat, cranked up the engine and sped away.

Barlow watched the high-perched taillights of the truck disappear down the blacktop road and savored the many ways he might dispose of his superfluous partner when the deal was through. He had no intention of allowing the spineless Miller to walk away scotfree after the things he'd said. Stars twinkled down on the now deserted roadside park along a forlorn stretch of Texas highway as Donald Barlow stood staring into the inky night. *Yes, once you've served your purpose, Miller, it'll a pleasure to break your worthless neck.*

Out of habit, he reached into his shirt pocket and withdrew a piece of his favorite English toffee. Single-handedly unfolding the square of dull silver paper, he channeled his thoughts away from his soon-to-be unnecessary confederate to the business at hand.

The weapon.

He plopped the candy into his mouth and took a long draw of its sweetness. Just remembering the feel of the cold metal against his palm, knowing the destructive capability the gun possess, excited him. So small to be so deadly.

By themselves, lasers were old hat. What made the Reese product unique was the power pack. For years, the energy required to operate lasers over five watts was contained in bulky and stationary housings. But now, the army's newest toy had brought an end to all that. Approximately the size of a traditional .45-caliber automatic pistol, the gun fired a ruby laser more powerful than the force of a hundred .45s. Lightweight, portable, the size of a jogger's cassette player, the power unit designed by Reese Defense Systems weighed less than a pound

9

and clipped to a man's belt. Together, such potency and mobility made the laser pistol and its operator an awesome, destructive force above and beyond imagination.

Barlow figured the Russians weren't far behind with the same technology, so selling the plans would bring only a pittance compared to what he could get for the tested, operational model. He had to strike while he had the advantage. Already, buyers were prepared to pay dearly for even one of the guns. With the money from this venture as investment capital, he would be set for a long time to come. No more dark roadsides, no more bowing and scraping to the money men of the world. He would be a rich man, demanding others bow to him. And nothing, and no one, was going to get in his way. His goals were set and this was the prime time for him to make his move. He must have the cash from the lasers to move forward with his other plans. Everything hinged on this deal.

Unexpectedly, a familiar excitement shot through his body. *Just like back in Nam. Those first few deals — scared to death but higher than a kite. If it hadn't been for . . .* Thoughts of his days in Vietnam were inevitably mixed with the name of one man. *Drew Kenyon.*

If it hadn't been for Kenyon, he'd be knee-deep in Swiss bank accounts by now. But no, Kenyon had to play hero — had to dig through the barrel until he found the rotten apple. Nothing could spoil the reputation of the precious Special Services.

"Because of you, Kenyon, I spent years living underground like a rat," Barlow spat at his absent enemy. "But soon, ole buddy, very soon, we'll be even."

Symbolically, Barlow's fist tightened around the slip of silver candy wrapper for a second before he tossed it into the cool Texas breeze.

Chapter 1

Treason, criminals, courtrooms. Drew Kenyon was sick of the words — sick of having to deal with them. The popular term was burnout. Whatever the name, he'd reached his limit. This was the last time for him, and it had come none too soon.

His gaze roamed over the contents of his attaché case. The files, notepads and endless pieces of paper required to do his job seemed to mock him. At that moment the cab driver took a corner without reducing speed and the attaché, propped nonchalantly on his widespread knees, pitched to one side and threatened to dump the loathsome documents. He snapped the bag closed and tossed it onto the seat beside him.

Three more days and the current case would be put to bed. Then he could finalize the law partnership and the move from Washington to New Orleans. Lean fingers worked over the vinyl armrest of the cab as though it were a worry stone. Stability. He needed some stability in his life, needed to get himself back into the mainstream of a "normal" existance. But he wasn't sure what normal was anymore. In the past, the norm of his life had been anything but sedate, much less stable. Too many years with no permanent address and only superficial friendships had made him a loner. Originally, he had chosen to be alone. Professionally, solitude suited him. Personally, it was almost a necessity. Few women were interested in a part-time relationship. He couldn't and never had blamed them. But lately, the loneliness had become a gnawing ache, eating away at him bit by bit.

The taxi screeched to a halt. Drew paid the fare, overtipping the driver, and with an air of resignation, strode into the Dallas Federal Courthouse. By the time he stepped off the elevator at the sixteenth floor, he was fully into his usual "prepresentation" mental hype, but his heart just wasn't in it this time. Stopping at a water fountain, he attempted to regroup his thoughts.

Absently, he stooped to take a drink of water. The clicking sound of high heels on tile grew louder, then faded as a woman passed him. He straightened slowly and took a deep breath.

A totally feminine and startlingly seductive fragrance filled his nostrils. Inhaling fully, he savored the enticing scent. Courtrooms and cases were momentarily relegated to the back of his mind and he inhaled again, capturing the last tiny traces of the indefinable, intriguing fragrance.

When was the last time a woman's perfume had drawn his attention? He couldn't remember. The realization was followed closely by a sharp pang of loneliness. Another block in the pyramid of his life that needed restructuring. He shook his head as if to clear it. Whatever the original fragrance, he decided the woman's own essence must have enhanced the commercial variety, because the lingering smell was unique.

His head automatically swiveled in search of the source of the alluring scent. His twilight-blue eyes unerringly spotted a rapidly receding, shapely figure and widened in appreciation. He liked what he saw.

The woman's walk was brisk but gracefully self-assured, the gentle sway of her hips naturally seductive. A tan dirndl skirt flatteringly displayed what he so obviously admired — not so loose as to detract from her near-perfect proportions, but not so tight as to appear blatant. Methodically, his appreciative gaze traveled to long, slender legs accentuated by immaculately polished, high-heeled navy pumps.

Drew's blue eyes sparkled as they slid back up the well-shaped limbs and nicely-rounded derriere to a narrow back covered by a classically tailored navy blazer. A cascade of rich sable-brown hair swung about her shoulders as she walked. The thick, burnished tresses fell in casual curls and waves that, he decided, begged to be crushed in a man's hands. He summed up the parts and found the whole definitely eye-appealing.

Though he'd only been granted a posterior view, instinct told him the front would be just as sensational, if not better. He wished she would turn just long enough for him to get a good look. . . .

As if to confirm his assessment, the woman rounded the corner at the end of the hall. Her right arm, swinging with the gentle rhythm of her step, inadvertently brushed back the unbuttoned jacket, allowing a fleeting glimpse of high, full breasts. A slight turn of her head revealed a delicate cheekbone and a creamy complexion before she disappeared.

Drew had an unexpected, unexplainable urge to follow her. It was more than just to see a beautiful woman. And he knew she was beautiful. Just as he knew her voice would be soft and sexy. The mystery lady had more than taken his thoughts away from the impending presentation; she had captured his imagination. Annoyed with his uncharacteristic daydreaming, he checked his watch: 8:53. No time to — He stopped himself abruptly. Had he actually been about to follow her? He quickly dismissed the idea and forced his thoughts to the business at hand.

Gripping his camel-colored leather attaché, he started off in the opposite direction. Long, purposeful strides took him down the hall and through a set of double wooden doors. The sign proclaimed in bold white letters etched in black plastic: UNITED STATES FEDERAL ATTORNEY'S OFFICE, NORTHERN DISTRICT OF TEXAS.

Laine Stewart rounded the corner and hastened her step,

unmindful of the people she passed. Damn, she hated to be late. Tardiness was one of her pet peeves. For the dozenth time in the past hour, she cursed the careless drivers who chose this morning to get involved in a three-car accident on the inbound side of the Central Expressway. Luckily there were no injuries, but the ensuing traffic jam had been monumental. Laine glanced at the slim gold watch on her wrist: 8:55. With five minutes to spare, she sailed into the federal grand jury room and heard a click as the door locked behind her.

Walking directly to the farthermost of two rectangular tables dominating the room, she hurriedly greeted the deputy foreman with a warm handshake and a quick smile. Still chafing at her own tardiness, she sank into her designated chair and plunked her handbag on the floor.

Glancing around the austere but spacious jury room, Laine took a fast head count. No need to worry about reaching a quorum of seventeen today. Easily, twenty of the twenty-three members were present, which meant the voting would take longer. As usual, they would be confined for three days and Laine could ill afford the time. After almost eighteen months, the interruptions in her busy schedule every fifth week still left her feeling hassled. This latest notice had forced her to postpone a much-needed vacation. At times, doing one's civic duty could be a real pain in the posterior. Laine doubted that anyone in the room would disagree.

Impaneled over a year ago, the eclectic collection of individuals had gained a well-earned reputation for their efficient, no-nonsense processing of cases. The assiduous group was thorough and concise in its questions and deliberations. In the previous session alone, twenty-seven indictments had been handed down in a single day, enabling the local police to dissolve a drug ring. And the small gathering of civic-minded citizens had helped bring the case to a satisfying conclusion,

14

Laine thought proudly. They were, quite simply, ordinary people doing an extraordinary job.

Routinely, Laine flipped open a file containing a schedule of the cases to be heard and handed to the girl on her right a sheet of legal-size paper listing the names of the jurors.

"Good morning, Donna. Ready to get this show on the road?"

Donna Marshall, recording secretary for the grand jury, turned her attention from her romance novel to Laine. "Might as well. . . ."

A light tap on the door interrupted the conversational hum within the room as the familiar figure of Nelda Patterson was admitted.

"Good mornin'." The matronly aide to the vast staff of federal prosecutors addressed the jurors in a soft drawl as she advanced across the room. "I know y'all are eager to begin, but there's been a change in this mornin's schedule. Your first case was supposed to be one of Mr. Logan's but —" she paused, coming to stand beside Laine and point a lacquered nail to the first section of the file "— this case has been postponed. A much more pressing investigatory matter is to be presented. A federal prosecutor on special assignment from Washington will be arriving shortly. Here's the amendment to the schedule," Nelda added, placing a sheaf of legal documents on the table. "I think y'all will find this an interesting case to start your day with. 'Bout ten more minutes or so, and we'll be ready to begin."

"Thanks. Meanwhile we'll call the roll and determine the count and the number of certificates required," Laine responded.

"That's fine, dear." The woman patted Laine's arm in a maternal gesture. "I'll see you at the break."

As Nelda Patterson left the room, Laine returned her attention to Donna and nodded for her to proceed. The secretary rose and cleared her throat.

"Okay, folks, sing out as I call your names and tell me if you need certificates of attendance for you employers."

As Donna's voice ceased a few minutes later, Ruth Jackson, one of the jurors, waved a folded copy of the *Dallas Morning News* in Laine's direction. "Did you see the article in the paper about our drug case?"

"No, I didn't." Laine rose and walked to join the group of jurors at the table nearest the door. "But I'm always intrigued to read the newspaper reports on how well we did our job." She stopped directly in front of Ruth and rested her hip on the edge of the table as she accepted the paper.

"Sure was a big bust." Ruth's comment was followed by nods of agreement from surrounding jurors.

A retired dentist seated across from Ruth chimed in, "Makes you kinda proud when you know you've been instrumental in helping get that stuff off the streets and out of the reach of kids."

"Yeah, it's a good feeling. Even if we only make a small dent, it's a start, right?" Ron Talbot, seated next to the dentist, substantiated.

"Amen," Laine agreed, hiking her skirt daintily as she half leaned, half sat on the corner of the table.

"Still," Ruth said with a sigh, "with all we've done, sometimes it galls me to think we can't say a word about what goes on in this room. Yet, I'm always amazed at how much information the newspaper has. Every time I come home from one of these sessions, my husband always asks if we 'sent anybody up the river.' " She giggled and shook her head. "I keep telling him we only indict, we don't convict."

"Know what you mean," the dentist reiterated. "I think a lot of people don't have any idea how the grand jury works. I

16

know I didn't. Bet some lawyers don't even know we serve for eighteen months, or that service can't be postponed."

"Sometimes I just crave to tell my husband about some of our cases, but I have to bite my tongue," a young housewife beside Ruth interjected. "So you know what I do?" Her voice lowered conspiratorially. "When I see a piece in the paper about a case we heard, I bring it to his attention. It's a little game we play. That way, I haven't actually told him a thing." Good-natured laughter followed and agreement that their vows of secrecy were sometimes put to the acid test.

"Anything juicy on today's agenda?" Ruth asked.

Laine shrugged. "We'll see. Some special prosecutor from Washington is coming in. Must be important, if they're bringing in the big guns from up north." She smiled and the conversation drifted, spreading out among the jurors. Laine began a quick scan of the newspaper article.

Absorbed in her reading, she didn't look up immediately when another knock sounded at the door and a juror responded. Suddenly the hair on the back of Laine's neck prickled, and intuitively she knew that it was not Nelda Patterson who had entered the room. She lifted her chin and looked straight into the most unusual blue eyes she had ever seen. They were azure, clear and sparkling, and . . . downright mesmerizing.

The newcomer stood six feet plus, broad shouldered, but not beefy. With casual elegance he wore a navy pinstripe three-piece suit. The leather attaché case held in one hand echoed his excellent taste in attire. His other hand was shoved deep into a trouser pocket, the forearm holding back one side of his coat. He stood tall and straight, feet planted slightly apart; the stance emphasized his muscular thighs and the slimness of his hips. Traces of Nordic lineage had etched his face — strong, rugged and definitely sensual.

17

Even though his square jaw and firm mouth bespoke stubbornness, when his lip curled, as it did now, with just a hint of a smile, she suspected it was more characteristic of confident determination. He possessed an air of authority and virility that shouted *man* from the top of his thick, tawny-gold hair right down to his expensive-looking Italian shoes.

The expected Washington, D.C., prosecutor had obviously arrived! What she found *unexpected* was her reaction to the man. Heart thumping, Laine was suddenly filled with an inexplicable, quiet joy — as though she had been marching out of step in a lifelong parade and, all at once, was in perfect unison with the world around her. It was an eerie yet welcome feeling. Goose bumps danced across her shoulders and down her arms. Subconsciously, Laine began to rub her upper arm. The newcomer's gaze dropped to follow the movement of her fingers, traveled up and over narrow shoulders, then returned steadfastly to her eyes.

Laine was staring in open appraisal; and the realization jolted her. Chagrined, she cleared her throat and slid from her position with as much dignity as she could muster — not an easy feat since she had practically draped herself over the table. Out of the corner of her eye, she noted with embarrassment that the hint of a smile on the man's handsome face had grown into a full-fledged grin.

Drew watched her slip smoothly from the table and walk away. Pent-up air hissed from his lungs through even, white teeth in a long breath. He couldn't believe his good fortune when he entered the jury room and came face-to-face with the seductively perched figure. In a flash, his eyes mapped her body from the crown of lustrous brown hair, across a well-turned hip, over a crossed leg where the hem of her skirt was enticingly elevated to just above the knee. Full breasts strained against the white silk blouse tucked into the narrow waist of her skirt — a waist that would fit the span of his hands perfectly. He was right: the front not only equaled but surpassed the back.

The vision was indelibly etched in his brain, but he had no intention of filing it away in his storehouse of memories. Venus had vanished and reappeared . . . . and Drew Kenyon did not believe in tempting fate.

But fate could be heartless. The obvious fact of who and what they were hit him full force. He was a federal prosecutor, and she, no matter how attractive, was a federal grand juror. He could look, but he couldn't touch.

Truth be known, this was not the first speech of self-denial Drew had ever delivered to himself. In instances past, when experiencing a similar attraction toward a jury member, he had always been able to dismiss it with a "Too bad" shrug. But this time, he didn't want to dismiss the young woman whose very presence he could feel from across the room, even though she was not in his line of vision. Briefly, desire played devil's advocate against his better judgment. Damn, he groaned inwardly, then turned to address the gathering.

"Good morning, ladies and gentlemen. My name is Andrew Kenyon. I'm a special prosecutor from Washington, D.C." His rich baritone voice was as clear as his eyes. His hand reached to smooth his tie, fingertips unconsciously grazing a line from the middle of his chest to a spot just above his belt.

"I very much appreciate your time today, especially at the last minute." He offered the jurors his best gosh-I'm-just-tickled-to-be-here smile. "I'm glad to know Southern hospitality is still extended warmly to those of us who live above the Mason-Dixon line." Faint laughter twittered through the room. Drew's eyes met Laine's and held for a moment before he continued.

"The case I'll be presenting is an investigatory one . . . thus

19

far. Eventually, we'll be seeking indictments on several targets, but today will consist primarily of the testimony of a government witness. His testimony should provide us with a strong base for our proposed indictment. I cannot reveal all the facts as yet, but I can tell you this is a matter involving national security and high treason." He allowed the words to settle in, giving him time to gauge the jury's reaction.

Laine's attention, as well as that of every other juror, was now riveted on the prosecutor.

"I don't think I need remind the members of the grand jury of their oath of secrecy, but I will say that the witness you are about to hear is testifying at considerable personal risk. The target of the grand jury is unaware of our investigation. Should even a whispered rumor reach our suspect, millions of dollars and several lives would be in jeopardy." He paused again and glanced down at the file in his hand. "Madam Foreman . . . Ms. Stewart, I believe." He checked the roster for the proper name before scanning the faces for acknowledgment. Again, his search ended when he made eye contact with Laine.

"Y—yes," Laine answered, so concerned with her own reactions to Prosecutor Kenyon that she completely missed the look of surprise in the blue eyes, a look quickly followed by one of regret.

"With your permission —" he gave a curt nod "— I'll call the witness."

"Certainly."

Drew turned and walked to the door. Venus wasn't just a grand juror, but the foreman! He plucked a nonexistent piece of lint from his lapel and frowned. She was so far out of his reach, she might as well be the evening star.

Politely Drew ushered in the witness while reining his wayward thoughts. Returning to his place, his frown deepened as it occurred to him that his objectivity regarding the foreman was listing badly. What was there about Laine Stewart that made him want to break the rules for the first time? He sought but found no logical answer. He only knew that this time was different — and the knowledge was more than slightly disconcerting.

Laine's naturally silky voice drifted across the room, reminding Drew of his earlier prediction. "Do you swear that the testimony you are about to give this grand jury is the truth, the whole truth, so help you God?"

"I do," came the witness's firm reply.

The court reporter's fingers flew across the keys of her machine as Drew began his questioning.

"Will you state your name and occupation for the grand jury?" Drew inquired.

"Thomas Collier. I'm an agent for the Central Intelligence Agency, on an undercover assignment." At his words an intense quiet settled over the room.

"Will you tell the members of the grand jury the nature of that assignment?" Drew's voice was smooth, firm, quietly commanding.

"To act as go-between for the sale of valuable government property to a foreign power."

"Could you be specific? Just give the grand jury, in your own words, the pertinent events that have led up to the present."

"Yes, sir." The witness shifted in his chair. "To begin with, the army has developed a very sophisticated laser weapon that can be installed in helicopters, jet fighters, almost any kind of air or surface craft. With minimum modification, it can also be used as a sidearm." Obviously inexperienced with having to appear before a jury, the agent paused and squirmed in the hard chair before continuing. Nervously, he looked around the room and linked his hands together in his lap.

21

"I'm sure this must sound like Star Wars to some of you, but it is real. And the laser weapon was developed in Dallas by Reese Defense Systems. A limited number of the guns were tested, then stockpiled at their plant in San Antonio, under guard. But anytime you handle something like this, there's always a problem with maintaining security.

"Approximately two months ago, our agency received a tip from an anonymous informant that someone inside the Reese plant intended to sell some of these weapons to a government who's opposed to the ideals of the free world. My job was to make contact with the person in San Antonio and gain knowledge of the details of the sale and the name of the buyer." The agent cut his eyes to Drew. "These weapons are so new, the asking price is over a hundred thousand dollars . . . each." There were several audible gasps in the room.

"Naturally, we want to stop the sale, but we also want the buyer, a man named Donald Barlow. Barlow's a real rotten apple. You name it, he's involved — dope, guns, information — anything that brings a high dollar return; and he's not particular which side of the iron curtain he sells to. For years, Barlow has eluded capture. This time, we think we have him dead to rights."

Drew noted the jurors' reaction and one corner of his mouth quirked in a tiny smile. If they were shocked by the figures Collier had just quoted, Drew wondered what their response would be if he revealed just how much Barlow had cost the United States government over the past ten years — in dollars and lives. Collier's description of Barlow was apt: "a rotten apple," spoiling everything he touched.

"Are there any questions the jury wishes to ask this witness?" No hands were raised as Drew glanced around the room. "Thank you, Agent Collier. Would you be kind enough to wait outside?"

22

As soon as the door closed behind the witness, one of the elderly jurors used her hand.

"Mr. Kenyon, I do have a question, but it's not about the testimony."

"All right."

"I was curious about the witnesses. You know, the government agents that come in here. They all seem so nice and most of them are quite young. Yet their jobs read like something out of a spy novel. How do they keep up that kind of existence for years and not become . . . sort of jaded. Everyday life must seem dull in comparison."

The question was a familiar one. How many times had it been asked of him personally over the years? He smiled at the woman.

"They are simply law-enforcement officers, not unlike your own city policemen, only on a national and sometimes international scale. But you're correct in assuming the general public sees their jobs as being filled with high adventure and intrigue. Believe me, their lives can be as dull as yours or mine. As for their age, well, most of them burn out or want out after a few years. Very few agents are pensioned off."

"You sound as though you have firsthand knowledge of how the other half lives," the dentist commented.

Laine didn't miss the instantaneous tightening of the muscles in Drew's neck, or the way his gaze drilled the juror.

"Let's just say I received my information from a reliable source and let it go at that." Drew turned his head toward Laine and addressed her directly. "Could we take a coffee break?"

"Yes," Laine agreed, coming to her feet so quickly she was compelled to steady herself by gripping the edge of the table. "Please be back in fifteen minutes," she admonished, "at ten forty-five."

Immediately, bubbles of conversation bounced around the room. Laine heard mumbled can-you-believe-its and boy-this-is-going-to-be-a-humdingers, but the jurors were careful to change the subject of their conversations as they filed past the prosecutor's table on their way out of the room.

Passing within inches of Andrew Kenyon, Laine fought the urge to sneak a discreet look at him. She was about to celebrate victory over her baser instincts when the sound of his voice brought her up short.

"Ms. Stewart?"

"Yes?" A slow turn brought them face to face.

"I wonder if I might prevail upon Southern hospitality a bit further for directions to the snack shop. I'll return the favor and buy you a cup of coffee." Better judgment was forgotten as his twilight-blue eyes captured her hazel ones.

In a nervous gesture indicative of her indecision, Laine wet her lips. Drew's heart thudded and his stomach muscles involuntarily tightened as the pink tip of her tongue painted a glistening path along her mouth.

"Uh, no that won't be necessary, Mr. Kenyon." In the long silence as people filed past them, Drew and Laine stared, mindful only of each other.

"It's . . . it's on the eleventh floor," she finally stammered.

"What is?" he asked softly, still holding her prisoner with his eyes.

"The snack shop."

"Oh," he mouthed, then said aloud, "thanks."

"You're . . . welcome," Laine returned breathlessly, then beat a hasty retreat.

Five minutes later, Laine glanced up to see Andrew Kenyon enter the coffee shop. Was it her imagination or did he seem to stand head and shoulders above every other man in the room? The rest of the male occupants unquestionably paled in comparison to the tall blond attorney. Strangely, for the first time, Laine found herself giving more than a passing thought to the men around her. She didn't like this new awareness, nor did she like admitting to herself who was responsible for the change. Maybe he'll get his coffee and leave, she hoped. No such luck. Not only did Special Prosecutor Kenyon remain in the room, he walked straight to the table next to hers. Drew acknowledged the jurors with a warm smile and selected a chair that brought his back within inches of Laine's.

The Styrofoam cup shook in Laine's hand. Searching unsuccessfully for composure, Laine could have kissed the retired dentist seated across the table when he directed a question her way. "Still slaving away planning your convention, Laine?"

"Slaving is the right word." She responded with a smile of gratitude, her calm reply belying the trembling in her legs. The disturbing scent of a musky cologne seemed to dance across the air between Andrew Kenyon's body and hers. The smell was driving her to distraction, and she tapped the edge of her cup with a smooth, unpolished fingernail.

"How's it coming?" Kathy Brennan, a local bookstore owner, continued the line of conversation.

"Very well," Laine responded, gratefully diverting her thoughts. "I have some talented and industrious people working with me, but little snags keep popping up. As a matter of fact," she said a wry grin, "our jury session this week turned out to be one of those snags."

"I know what you mean," Kathy agreed. "Seems like the federal government has inside information as to when I'm going to get a huge shipment for my store. I get a call from the distributor asking me to pick up a ten-ton order and a notice for one of these sessions the same day. Never fails," she quipped, shaking her head. The rest of the group nodded and smiled in sympathetic accord.

"If it weren't for good ole Uncle Sam," Laine lamented, "I could be relaxing in the tropical sunshine of Cancún right now."

"Sounds like a dream come true to me . . . single, sun, fun!" Donna Marshall commented enviously. "Business or pleasure?"

"Both," Laine said with a smile. "Actually, some conference planning remains to be done with the Plaza Americana, but after that, I'm on vacation. Decided I might as well take advantage of the trip. I was scheduled to fly out this past Saturday, but —" she shrugged with resignation "— duty called."

"How long will you be in Mexico?" Dr. Howell inquired, peering over his thick-lensed glasses.

"Nine days in all. The first two I'll meet with the hotel staff and check out tours we'll be offering our conventioneers. After that —" Laine downed the last of her coffee and plopped the cup on the tabletop "— my time is my own, and *this* convention coordinator intends to soak up some sun and be waited on hand and foot for a week."

"Atta girl," Kathy said, "and take a bunch of pictures so we can all turn green with envy at the next session. That's probably as close to Cancún as I'll ever get." A round of laughter followed, then someone called attention to the time. Laine was still very much aware of Andrew Kenyon as he trailed the group from the coffee shop, and she purposefully stepped to the back of the elevator.

The session resumed with the same witness until lunchtime, then reconvened an hour later. Throughout the proceedings, Laine found it increasingly difficult to concentrate on the testimony. Her thoughts, not to mention her gaze, kept wandering to the handsome prosecutor as he systematically questioned the CIA agent. She tried to be attentive but found herself holding a silent interrogation of her own, like, was he married, engaged, or otherwise involved? How long would he be in town? What did he do when he wasn't working? Did he play tennis, jog or swim to keep that gorgeous body in shape?

Unexpectedly a vision materialized in Laine's head. A scene of Andrew Kenyon walking out of a foaming surf, clear, sparkling turquoise water in the background. Tight-fitting white trunks hugged his slim hips and saltwater glistened on his bare chest. Bright sunlight danced over his wet, golden head, portraying him a shining, bronzed Adonis. He came out of the water, walking straight toward her as she reclined on dazzling white sand . . . waiting. Slowly, he lowered himself beside her, until his tanned knees were embedded in the sand inches away from her scantily clad hips! The image was so real that Laine could almost smell the salt breeze from the ocean, hear the waves lapping against the warm sand, feel the touch of his equally warm breath as he leaned ever closer, his handsome head inches from hers. Seawater ran in rivulets down his face, and her throbbing, overly sensitive fingertips twitched with the need to reach out and halt a drop trickling toward his marvelous mouth.

A nerve-grating squeak, followed by the dull thud of a hardback book as it hit the floor, brought Laine crashing back to reality. Involuntarily she shuddered. Horrified to find herself staring at the object of her daydream, she quickly looked away. But not before Drew caught her expression. Their gazes met across the room and the endearing hint of a smile twitched at the corner of his mouth.

God, the man must think she was sending him an open invitation, the way she'd been leering. *Well, haven't you?* a small voice inside her ridiculed. There was no hope of containing the red flush creeping up her neck to stain her cheeks. She

27

bent her head and made a show of taking notes that she knew would probably resemble hieroglyphics later.

Drew's head started to spin when he looked up and saw Laine watching him, barely hidden fires of passion flaring in her eyes. Never in his life had he witnessed such open desire on a woman's face . . . in public . . . and directed solely at him. A look that said the rest of the world had disappeared, leaving them completely alone in a vacuum of their own desire. Rattled, he almost stumbled over his next two questions. He tried not to look at her, but he couldn't help himself.

Drew gave a derisive shake of his head, but the sexual awareness between them could not be denied. The tension exerted a powerful magnetic push-pull on the two unwilling participants. Even as they concentrated on their respective jobs, each was pointedly aware of the other.

Laine thought the afternoon break would never arrive. The minutes seemed to crawl by like dismal, rainy days. Finally, the witness's words ceased. Laine breathed a sigh of relief as Drew rose from his chair and tossed his pencil to one side of the desk.

"Thank you, Agent Collier. Your testimony has been quite comprehensive. Does the grand jury have any questions for the witness?" Drew's gaze scanned the faces of the jurors before stopping at Laine's. "Madam Foreman, since there are no further questions for this witness, may he be excused?"

"Yes." Laine was glad the uncomfortable day was drawing to a close. As the agent left the room, Drew closed the well-used file folder and slipped it into his attaché case. In a smooth, formal voice he addressed the jurors.

"I would like to thank the grand jury for your patience. I appreciate your making room for me in an already crowded schedule." His words indicated the presentation was finished, but he didn't leave immediately. He dallied just long enough so that some of the jurors must have felt the need to make conversation.

"How do you like Texas?" a man inquired.

"I like it better each time I visit," Drew said, cutting his eyes to Laine's table.

"Bet you'll be glad to get back to the cooler Washington temperatures," the juror said with a grin. "Texas in August can be murder on you Yankees."

"It has been hotter than I expected." Drew cleared his throat, then commented teasingly, "But Washington isn't exactly the north pole, you know."

The juror, a transplanted Yankee himself and a former New York City cab driver, eyed the prosecutor judiciously. "You don't talk like you're a D.C. native. I'd say —" the ex-cabbie calculated "— Midwest. Des Moines maybe, or K.C."

"St. Louis," Drew validated. "You have a good ear." The juror returned a self-satisfied smile.

"Have you been to Dallas before?" Ruth Jackson joined in the polite probing.

"A few times. I do a lot of traveling."

"I bet your wife doesn't like that," Ruth deduced.

"If I had one, she probably wouldn't," Drew said pointedly, not bothering to see if Laine were paying any attention to the conversation. He knew she was. Unceremoniously, and without a backward glance in Laine's direction, Drew collected his files, again offered his appreciation and left the grand jury room.

Even though Laine told herself she was glad not to have Andrew Kenyon in the same room for the rest of the day, when the session reconvened she was restless and vaguely discontented. Perhaps, she tried to convince herself, the case being presented now was dull and colorless in contrast to the Washington prosecutor's. If that were true, then why did she repeatedly look at the middle-aged attorney reading an indictment, wishing he were tall, blond and broad shouldered?

Shortly after five o'clock Laine exited from the federal courthouse, still berating herself for allowing Andrew Kenyon to unsettle her. She crossed the street to the parking lot and unlocked her car door, leaving it open in order to release the trapped, hot August air. Unexpectedly, the hair at the back of her neck bristled and she knew it had nothing to do with the late-afternoon heat. Slowly, Laine looked back toward the front of the courthouse.

Looking cool and relaxed, Andrew Kenyon stood facing the parking lot, apparently in conversation with another man. His words may have been directed at the man in front of him, but his eyes were only for Laine. His scrutiny was unnerving. Cold chills danced up Laine's spine as she quickly jerked her head around and scrambled inside her hunter-green Skylark, suddenly welcoming its overheated, stifling confinement.

Ten minutes later she was in the middle of rush-hour traffic, grateful for the diversion. Handling bumper-to-bumper congestion, one-hundred-degree temperatures and short-tempered drivers were all a snap compared to dealing with the turmoil she experienced whenever her thoughts returned to a certain attractive prosecutor.

Chapter 2

With one exception, the following day was a repeat of the previous one. Laine was mad — furious with herself for reacting so strongly to a total stranger, a man she'd never seen before and, most likely, would never see again after tomorrow. Even more enraging was her inability to shake the influence of the encounter.

She'd slept fitfully, finally waking a full hour before her alarm was set to go off. Unable to go back to sleep, she'd decided to use the extra time to be lazy, read the morning paper, have three cups of coffee instead of her usual one. But had she? No! Instead, the additional minutes were squandered plowing though her wardrobe for exactly the right dress, just the right accessories. She'd taken more time with her makeup and her hair than usual. The results had been gratifying and infuriating; Laine had alternately fumed and fretted on the drive to the courthouse. Now, she almost stomped from the parking lot to the coffee shop across the street from the courthouse for her customary coffee-to-go.

This is asinine! She tapped her foot with irritation as she waited in line at the counter. *Twenty-nine years old, the ill effects of a bad marriage still fresh in your mind, and you go absolutely critical over some smooth, blond, good-looking . . . Yankee carpetbagger!* The Southern expression of disdain seemed to be the only negative she could apply to a man who in every other way appeared to be ideal. Laine almost laughed aloud at the old-fashioned label; but then, she was an old-fashioned woman.

That was part of her problem, or so her ex-husband had told her. She remembered how shocked she'd been to discover that their income was more dependent on the legs of some horse or a quarterback's arm than on her husband's consulting business; and how angry he'd been at her request to try a more honest way to make a living. She could still hear the hateful tone in Greg Stewart's voice as he ranted over how her morals were outdated and prudish. Was it outdated to expect fidelity of a husband of only one a year? Was it prudish to insist on dissolving the marriage once she discovered that not only had he been unfaithful, repeatedly, but bragged about it openly among his gambling friends? Laine still felt the hurt and anger over the bitter divorce, and the rejection and loneliness when it was all over.

No! Laine shook her head, causing brown curls to dance about her shoulders. She couldn't, wouldn't live like that. What she and Greg had together hadn't been a marriage. As far as Laine was concerned, the relationship had been a downhill slide into self-degradation and she thought too much of herself to allow the same situation to happen ever again. Laine's bitterness over the trauma of her divorce had faded, leaving a very cautious lady in its wake. She dated occasionally, but selectively. Although possessing a healthy appreciation for a good-looking man, she liked her life the way it was: orderly and unencumbered. A head-over-heels, purely physical relationship had no place in her life right now. Yet, for all her bravado, Greg Stewart's sharp words had helped germinate a tiny seed of self-doubt and sometimes, in those half-waking predawn hours, Laine's subconscious fear of failure grew.

Unbidden thoughts of the tawny-haired Andrew Kenyon intruded and Laine recalled her uncharacteristic response to him. Well, she'd been anything but prudish yesterday! She was positively drooling over the man by the end of the day — and he knew it. A federal prosecutor, no less! But her attraction to him represented more than just a compromising situation.

For Laine Stewart, who professed to want only the most

orderly and sedate of life-styles, Andrew Kenyon was a threat.

She had sensed it immediately, but the warning signals had somehow gotten all mixed up with the sexual ones. Now, in the cold light of day, she could identify the disturbing vibrations. *Danger!* Only a touch, but it had been there, in his eyes, his body language. The instant a comment had been made about his having firsthand knowledge about an agent's life, he'd honed in on it, almost defensively. The moment she had laid eyes on Andrew, Laine had sensed he wasn't the run-of-the-mill grand jury prosecutor. He was too smooth, almost blasé, with an aura of seasoned nonchalance. One didn't acquire the kind of sophistication he possessed working for the government — at least not as a prosecutor.

Laine had had enough of dashing worldly types to last her a lifetime. What she wanted was a man with both feet planted solidly, eight to five, no adventure, secure. The last thing she needed was to fall for a refugee from the fast lane. Experience had taught her that a man, once exposed to that kind of life, never lost a taste for it. No, Andrew Kenyon was definitely off-limits! Laine shook her head, mentally posting a No Trespassing sign around the handsome prosecutor's neck as she exited the restaurant and dashed to obey the flashing green Walk sign on the corner.

She was still busy berating herself as she stepped into the jury room. The first person she saw was Andrew Kenyon and instantly all her resolve was for naught.

His suit was light gray-blue, a shade that matched his eyes to the color of a summer sky. If possible, he was even more attractive than she remembered. And just as dangerous. Even so, she could hardly take her eyes from him. Damn the man, Laine groaned inwardly. He could probably wear rags and still look regal.

The assessment proved to be prophetic when, for the rest

of the day, Laine found herself mentally attempting to dress him in tattered clothes. But the only image that materialized was one of him with a rumpled bed-sheet draped seductively around his naked body. The picture did nothing to ease her heightened sensitivity.

What was the matter with her? She seemed to have a one-track mind where this man was concerned, leading straight to . . . Where was she headed with all this nonsense? She was acting as if she'd never seen an attractive man before. *You're working too hard. Stress, deadlines, too much pressure. You absolutely, positively, need a vacation!*

How do you take a vacation from loneliness?

What a strange question, she thought. She wasn't the least bit lonely. Or was she? She enjoyed having time to herself. Didn't she? Try as she might, when she attempted to picture herself alone, a Nordicly handsome man hovered in the background of her mind. Absurd! Her nerves couldn't handle this kind of woolgathering.

What Laine didn't know was that Drew's thoughts unerringly paralleled hers. Each time he caught her eye his chest constricted and breathing became difficult. He knew he was way out of line with this one — his career, not to mention endless hours of work and tax-payers' money, could go up in smoke if he even *thought* of getting involved with a juror. Throw in a possible jail sentence and he had all the ingredients of a real disaster.

Logical, realistic approaches to any given situation were the cornerstone of Drew Kenyon's existence. Yet, his reaction to Laine Stewart defied all logic and the realization relentlessly gnawed at him.

The afternoon session seemed interminable as time and time again Laine felt Andrew Kenyon watching her. Unobtrusively she glanced around the room, attempting to gauge whether or not any of the jurors had noticed his visual assessment. The man was phenomenal! How could he watch her like a cat eyeing a bowl of cream and not miss a beat as he fired question after question at the witness? *Damn him!*

By now she was ready to damn him for anything and everything — especially for the one thing she reciprocated: the rushing stream of desire that coursed between them like a flood-swollen river threatening to overflow its banks. The sensation was awesome, frightening. Yet, strangely, as the afternoon wore on, Laine began to come to terms with her feelings, accepting them, albeit grudgingly. Acceptance did not lessen the tension, but did make it easier to bear; the truth was unavoidable.

She *wanted* Andrew Kenyon — wanted him in a way she had never wanted a man before. Laine was experiencing pure, basic lust and knew without a doubt that he returned the feeling. She wanted to feel the texture of his bare chest beneath her fingers, taste the honeyed warmth of his mouth — wanted it all. The fact that he possessed a touch of danger only intensified her longing. Perhaps, she reasoned, the attraction lay in the fact that he was off-limits, that she could fantasize without fear of reproach.

As she sat watching his cool, professional performance, the realization slowly dawned upon her that nothing could come of her desires and amorous fantasies. The No Trespassing sign became a comfort instead of a barrier. There was simply no way for any of her dreams to become reality. He was out of reach. The consequences of a federal prosecutor becoming involved with a member of the grand jury were not trivial and they were both aware of the fact. Involvement would be catastrophic, therefore unthinkable.

She felt relatively safe. An unexpected sense of recklessness stole over Laine. Her sexual daydreams could be enjoyed to the limit with no fear of losing control of the situation. Why not? Deliberately, with malice aforethought, Laine looked directly at him. Allowing her eyelids to droop slightly, she smiled. Her glossy lips formed a deliciously seductive curve.

Drew glanced up to find lustrous pink lips smiling at him, open desire flashing in liquid gold-flecked bedroom eyes. A shaky stomach did handsprings as his mouth went bone-dry. Had he been asking questions at that moment, he would have been hard-pressed to maintain his train of thought. *God Almighty, she may as well stand up in front of everyone here and ask me to meet her at the nearest hotel. What the hell does she think she's doing?*

Her blatantly sexy smile was undermining his control and he fought a surge of sweet anger. *She's driving me to distraction, that's what she's doing!*

In fact, she'd driven him further than to mere distraction. That very morning, curiosity about Laine's marital status had compelled him to ask for the sheet of information filed on each juror. The request, although completely ethical, was not Drew's style. The form contained personal data he considered private and therefore to be handled carefully. How many times had he rationalized his request to himself? How long had he debated before admitting the truth? He wanted to know everything about Laine Stewart.

Desire for information about a woman had never been strong enough for him to push his own personal code of ethics so far. It was now. A distinct possibility existed that his code would be sorely tested before his job was finished. From where he stood, the risk was worth taking. His biggest problem at the moment was battling her seduction by design. Turnabout, he decided, was fair play. Looking straight into Laine's glowing hazel eyes, he gave as good as he got — sending her a lingering look and slow smile designed to melt a woman's defenses at fifty paces.

The session ended and Laine's attempted quick getaway was not quick enough. Drew caught up with her at the elevator.

"Ms. Stewart?" *Thought you were home free, didn't you?* his eyes taunted.

"Yes," Laine said, quickly masking her surprised expression.

"I understand you are the lady to see if I want information about hotels."

"I beg your pardon?" She swallowed hard and stared at him.

"New Orleans . . . a place to stay? One of the jurors told me you're a wealth of information regarding hotels. I have to present a case in New Orleans next month and thought you might be able to suggest a comfortable but reasonable hotel," he concluded in a businesslike manner. *Flimsy, Kenyon, very flimsy. She'll never go for it.*

"Oh, I see." The pink in her cheeks sprang to life, partly from the tone of his question, but mostly from the idea that he had been interested enough to learn something about her. The thought thrilled her and at the same time caused her more concern. No matter how innocent, theirs wasn't a casual encounter and they both knew it.

He'd purposely stepped away from the bank of elevators after he'd first gained her attention and unknowingly she'd followed until they were well removed from eavesdropping ears.

"I'm sorry," he apologized, as though he were just realizing the obvious implications of his question. "I hope you didn't misconstrue my meaning. Someone mentioned you recently arranged a convention in New Orleans and I thought you might be able to steer me in the right direction."

He flashed his bone-melting smile and Laine began to have serious doubts about her ability to withstand his potent charm. Misconstrue, my aunt's fanny, she thought, fighting against the warmth of that damnable, delicious smile.

"You know, for all your Southern hospitality, we Yankees sometimes feel unwelcome, especially if we don't use the right approach . . . so to speak."

He was deliberately baiting her and enjoying every minute of it. Laine was tempted to tell him to take his bait and go fish in another pond. Women all over the world had probably fallen victim to his smooth style.

"I don't think you have to worry about your approach, Mr. Kenyon. You strike me as the kind of man whose intelligence and determination stand you in good stead wherever you go. You'd probably do very well without my help," she returned, feeling not a twinge guilty at having cut him off.

"Drew."

"What?"

"My friends call me Drew. And you're probably right, but I like to take advantage of a well-timed opportunity when it occurs. I've a dinner meeting later, but perhaps we could discuss this over a cup of coffee," he prompted, keeping his tone even.

"I don't think —"

"I can assure you, it's purely for business reasons. I'm not in the habit of making improper proposals to proper Southern ladies," he interrupted, with just the right amount of reproach coloring his voice.

Laine was diligently trying to find a logical way of saying no; she wasn't having much luck. After all, she reasoned, what harm could it do to help the man out? He merely wants the name of a good hotel. Her small internal voice sent back a "Don't kid yourself" message.

"You are, aren't you?" he broke her concentration.

"Aren't I what?"

"A proper Southern lady?" There was that smile again.

"Unquestionably." Just the tiniest hint of a responding grin played about her full lips. "That's one of the reasons I must decline. However —" she arched a brow to forestall another interruption "— I will be delighted to bring you some brochures. Then you can review them at your leisure and make a selection."

"Thank you." He was watching her lips move as she spoke and didn't have the vaguest idea how he responded, but it must have indicated that the conversation was closed because she turned back toward the elevator.

"Thank you," he stated again without enthusiasm.

She tossed him a crooked half smile over her shoulder. "You said that already." Then she stepped into the elevator.

"So I did." Drew shrugged sheepishly and watched her beautiful face and body disappear behind the closing elevator doors.

Drew rammed his hands into his pockets and stood very still for several moments. Let her go, he ordered himself, then admitted the order was invalid. A driving compulsion, stronger than any he had ever experienced, unreasonably demanded that he follow her.

Deep in thought, Laine walked from the courthouse into the bright sunlight, instinctively heading toward her car. The signal light at the corner barely commanded her attention as she stared absently down at her shoes, a frown wrinkling her brow. For the briefest moment, she thought she had seen genuine regret in Drew Kenyon's eyes, but she dismissed the possibility. He probably wasn't used to hearing the word "no" spoken in a feminine tone of voice. The light changed again while she pondered the encounter outside the elevator, and when she finally noticed the green signal, she changed her mind. Suddenly the solitude of her comfortable apartment didn't offer its usual appeal. On an impulse she chose not to examine too closely, Laine made her way down the block to a quiet lounge she knew served an above-average quiche and salad.

Fifteen minutes later she stared down at her food, unimpressed, her appetite waning. Oh well, she assured herself, at least it's better than . . . Than what? Than spending time with Drew Kenyon? With a resigned sigh, she jabbed a bite of quiche. Her hand froze with the fork scant inches from her mouth as she looked up and straight into the face of the man who so completely occupied her thoughts. Slowly, the fork lowered to clatter against the plate.

"May I join you?"

"No. I mean, should you? If anyone saw us together —"

"We'll indignantly claim to be victims of pure chance."

"Are we?"

"Hardly, but the law only requires you establish a reasonable doubt." He gave her a smile that redefined the word "charming."

"I'm not sure —"

"Call it a business dinner, if you like. I do need the name of a good hotel."

"I don't think anyone would believe this is a chance encounter, or a business dinner." She tried to sound stern, but self-restraint was waging a losing battle with emotion.

"And what do *you* believe?"

"That you followed me."

He shrugged. "It's a public restaurant. I saw you come in and decided that was all the recommendation I needed."

"And you think those elements qualify this as a coincidental meeting?"

"Circumstantial evidence." The smile faded and his voice lowered. "Please."

Did his voice *have* to sound so seductive?

"I suppose it is foolish to insist you sit at another table —"

she looked around helplessly "— particularly since they all seem to be taken." He had the good grace to grin sheepishly. In spite of herself she smiled at the obvious look of relief on his face.

The waitress appeared and Drew ordered a Scotch while Laine declined a refill of her wineglass. His nearness was all the intoxication she could handle. Drink in hand, he settled back in his chair as though it were the only place in the world he wanted to be. She noticed he didn't bother to order dinner.

"Did you want to stay in the French Quarter?" She wondered how long she could maintain a businesslike attitude with him sitting just across the table.

"I suppose so. Doesn't everyone?"

It was her turn to shrug. "No. Personally, I prefer the bed-and-breakfast establishments you find off the beaten paths."

"You like old cities, then?" For all the smoothness he had displayed a moment ago, his glib tongue seemed to have abandoned him.

"Yes, very much." She hadn't suffered such a conversational strain since junior high school.

"So do I. In fact, with the exception of making inane small talk with a beautiful woman, they're my favorite thing."

Laine looked up, a bit startled by his comment. Then they both laughed.

In the center of a cocktail napkin Drew twisted his glass back and forth. "Tell me about Laine Stewart."

"There isn't much to tell. I'm past twenty-one, a convention coordinator for a national restaurant chain, and —" she paused for emphasis "— foreman of a grand jury."

"Is that a subtle reminder?"

"Yes."

"Noted."

"Drew —"

41

"Your job sounds fascinating. Exactly what does a coordinator do besides recommend hotels to well meaning strangers?" God, the way she said his name was almost sinful. He toyed with the rim of his glasses and called himself several unprintable names for placing both of them in an uncomfortable position. But he just didn't seem to be able to stop himself. Every time he looked at her, his vow of self-control crumbled like a week-old cookie.

"Is this how you wear down your witnesses in court? By ignoring their side of the conversation?"

"If you think this is ignoring you, I must be slipping."

Laine shook her head and expelled a long sigh of exasperation. "Actually, I'm an assistant to the vice-president."

"And exactly what does an assistant to the vice-president do?"

"Everything from making coffee to executing a national convention for six hundred people from all over the world," Laine said without a hint of boastfulness.

"And you love all of it, don't you?" Drew finished understandingly.

Laine was absently swirling the ruby-red wine around her glass, and at his quiet statement she lifted contemplative nutmeg-colored eyes to study him intently before answering.

"Yes, I do. For all the hassle, headache and constant worry that everything won't all come off just right, I do love it. It's fun, exciting and very rewarding."

"And you do your job well." It wasn't a question but a statement of fact.

"Yes, I do," Laine confirmed. "But how did you know?"

"Elementary, my dear Watson." He laughed, the sound deep, warm and rich. "We attorneys are notorious for our ability to size up our opponents in a flash," he finished, twirling an imaginary handlebar moustache. He was trying to keep the conversation light, all the while wishing he could reach across the table and hold her hand.

"I wasn't aware you considered me an opponent," Laine said breathlessly, as she raised her glass to her lips and allowed the wine to slide down her throat.

Draw's eyes tracked the invisible path of the liquid until his hungry gaze rested on a spot between her breasts. He swallowed hard.

"I don't, but old habits die hard. I'm only trying to present my case as favorably as possible. You should have all the facts before you begin to deliberate. I'd hate for you to indict an innocent man on circumstantial evidence," he recommended in a velvety-rough voice.

Laine doubted seriously that there was anything circumstantial about Drew Kenyon. From where she sat, he looked very substantial indeed.

"How am I doing?" His voice lowered and softened.

She was a hung jury. Part of her wanted to tell him to go, that they were treading on dangerous ground. Another part, the most insistent part, wanted to tell him she was experiencing the same desire she saw in his eyes every time he looked at her.

"The jury is still out." She gave him a captivating if tentative smile and hurried to change the subject. "How long have you been a federal prosecutor?"

"A few years." This was not his favorite subject, but he decided he could handle the conversational detour if talking meant retaining the pleasure of her company. He reminded himself to keep it casual. "I went straight from law school to Vietnam. You might say I'm a long-standing employee of Uncle Sam."

The hesitation colored a tinge of bitterness and, coupled with Laine's growing suspicions, told her more than mere words.

"I didn't mean to pry."

"It's a natural question to ask of someone you don't know. I'm flattered you are intrigued."

"I wouldn't go so far as to say 'intrigued' —"

"Curious, then?"

"I'm not curious," she lied.

"Not even about my age, or my love life?"

"Certainly not!" Her feigned indignation missed the mark.

He chuckled. "I'm disappointed. Does that mean you're not interested enough to ask? Or merely shy?"

"Neither. This conversation is deteriorating."

"You started it." He shot her a devilish grin with a matching gleam in his eye.

Her responding shrug implied touché. "How old are you?"

"Too old for you."

"Now, just a min—"

"Thirty-six," he interrupted, all the humor suddenly gone from his voice. "Young enough to enjoy life, but mature enough to appreciate its finer moments . . . like today when I glanced up and saw the look in your eyes as you watched me."

Their gazes locked across the table and pretending became pointless. The air was static with electricity of their own formation. Sparks seemed to arc from her body to his, then back again.

"Do you know —" his voice dropped to almost a whisper, "— without trying, you're one of the most sensuous women I have ever met."

Laine's sharply indrawn breath hissed through the atmosphere. Oh Lord, she wanted to hear more, but it had to stop. She had to stop him before this went too far — before she lost the minuscule portion of willpower she still possessed and stepped into emotional quicksand.

"Please don't . . ."

"Does the truth bother you?" Huskiness lingered in his voice as it drifted across the space that separated them and played on her tightly strung nerves like a harpist.

"Yes — no! You shouldn't say things like that. We shouldn't even be here . . . together. . . ." Her voice died away.

"You're right, of course." Drew's crystal-blue gaze dropped to his half-empty glass and he released a sigh of resignation. Without looking at Laine he said, almost to himself, "But you're . . . You affect me in ways I'm not certain I understand."

"I . . . I have to go," she whispered, jumping up from the table. He knew he'd pushed her, and he cursed himself for his impatience.

"I'll walk you to your car," he offered quietly, coming to his feet and placing an assisting hand at her elbow. The contact shot through her like a jolt of electric current.

"No." Her voice was as unsteady as her nerves. "I . . . it's not necessary."

"It is for me. I can't let you walk away," Drew said with quiet emphasis, "without making sure you're safely locked inside your car." He didn't wait for her to repeat her refusal, but tossed a few bills on the table and purposefully guided Laine out of the lounge.

Walking beside him through the downtown streets as dusk seeped into night, Laine felt strangely removed from the city noise and grime. Was it her imagination, or was the fifteen-minute return walk to the parking lot taking more like thirty minutes? Or did Drew continually slow their pace, delaying their arrival? She cast sideways glances at him as they strolled along unhurriedly, marveling at the fact that the mere presence of the man beside her had the ability to transport her away from everyday thoughts and surroundings. She found herself succumbing like a drug addict who surrenders to that which he knows is life threatening, yet desires beyond all else.

And like an addict, she couldn't help herself. She was already hooked. A Drew Kenyon junkie. And she solemnly wondered if she would be able to kick the habit. *Stop it.* She overrode her meandering thoughts. She was only making matters worse. She had to get a grip on herself. *Thank him and walk away,* she told herself. *You can do it!*

But deep down, she knew she couldn't. She wanted him to kiss her, but knew if he did, she'd probably go to pieces — and one of them had to be strong.

They reached the car and as she bent to unlock the door, Laine held her breath. He didn't touch her . . . at least not then.

"Laine?" he breathed, her name a soft question on his lips.

Slowly, she straightened. As surely as if he had placed his hands on her shoulders and turned her to him, his voice touched her and she responded. Caught in a web of mutual desire, she was powerless to extricate herself. All Laine had to do was say good-night and mean it, but it was too late.

"Yes." Looking straight into Drew's compelling blue eyes, she didn't even pretend to misread the hunger she saw mirrored behind golden lashes. How could she deny a desire that matched her own? Nor did she attempt to move away when his head dipped toward her waiting lips. All her resolve, all her good intentions melted away as Drew's lips touched hers in a sweet, tender kiss, rife with restrained passion.

Like a burning cigarette tossed into a drought-stricken forest, hidden fires in the kiss smoldered, then burst into open flames. Like wildfire through dry timber, the conflagration leapt out of control and Laine and Drew were two helpless moths drawn inexorably to the blaze. Soft pink lips parted to receive Drew's hot, questing tongue. The action accompanied a deep groan as Drew pulled her into his arms and crushed her against him. Laine wound her arms inside his jacket and caressed the length of his back. Instinctively, her body arched toward his and she returned the kiss with impetuous abandon. One of his hands pressed the middle of her back, holding Laine fast, while the other roamed the enticing curve of her hip.

Finally, regretfully, Drew lifted his mouth from hers. In a voice thick and unsteady he whispered, "Laine, Laine . . . this is crazy." His large hands moved to gently cup her face.

"I know," she whispered, their breaths mingling, their lips only centimeters apart. "I never thought . . . never expected . . ."

"I know," he echoed, seeing the surprise mixed with longing reflected in her eyes. "Kiss me." His last words were a groan, smothered against her warm mouth.

The kiss was raw and urgent, as if he were trying to deny that this might be all there was for them — all there ever could be. Drew's strong fingers bit into the flesh of her upper arms and he suddenly thrust her away from him. His breath was hoarse and ragged.

"Oh Lord." He grated the words through clenched teeth, his eyes filled with a curious deep longing. "I can't seem to think past this minute, past the feel and taste of your mouth, the warmth of your body against mine." His brows drew together in an agony expression, as if he were in pain.

Drew shook his head decisively. "Now is not the right time. Just . . . drive away and don't look back. Please," he pleaded. "I'm not strong enough to walk away from you."

Dazed with arousal and stunned by his rejection, Laine responded like a robot programmed to obey her master's command. She backed away from him, her hazel eyes round and unblinking. With automated, jerky movements she opened the car door, slid inside, slammed it shut, inserted the key and started the engine. Shakily she slipped the gears into place and pressed her foot to the accelerator. She sensed the forward motion of the car, but the vehicle seemed to move on its own, not through any conscious directive from her.

Laine did not look back. By the time she reached the exit of the parking lot, a single tear had formed and trickled down her stoic face. She was halfway home before she became aware that her face was drenched with a deluge of tears.

Drew watched her drive away and raised his fist heavenward in angry frustration. *Dammit it to hell! Cupid's timing was lousy! Why now? Why her?*

The answers were irrelevant. What mattered was that she had touched him, touched his heart, and the loneliness had vanished. She made him feel alive, whole, and somehow renewed — a feeling too special to ignore.

He stood in the darkened parking lot for thoughtful moments, then turned on his heel. He knew what he had to do. Single-mindedly, he headed toward his hotel and a telephone. He gave little notice as the headlights of a car at the back of the parking lot winked into the night. The vehicle pulled into traffic several car lengths behind Laine's Buick.

Morning was unwelcome. The sunlight streaming through her bedroom window painfully pierced Laine's eyelids and she wished for a storm-darkened sky to fit her mood — bleak and depressing. She dreaded this day more than anything she had ever faced in her life. How on God's green earth would she get through the day looking at Drew, remembering the way he had kissed her, remembering the way she'd kissed him back?

Displaying willpower she would not have believed possible, Laine crawled from her bed and headed for the shower where the stinging spray revived body but not mind. She dressed without enthusiasm, gulped a tasteless cup of coffee and left, reluctant to face the ordeal ahead.

Laine Stewart waged a battle with herself every mile of the

drive downtown. The temperature had soared to ninety degrees by 8:30; traffic was a nightmare. Laine felt as though she had placed last in the Boston Marathon by the time she approached the door to the jury room. Hand poised to knock, for the briefest second Laine almost gave in to the urge to turn and run as fast as she could. When she was able to force her fist against the wooden door, knocking was unnecessary; the trembling did it for her. The door opened, she took a deep breath and stepped through.

Her gaze automatically went to the prosecutor's table, then widened in surprise. Laine stopped in midstride when she saw — not the man she expected — but a total stranger. Frantically, she glanced around the room. Drew Kenyon was nowhere to be seen.

The man at the table looked up from his notes and smiled benignly. Laine nodded acknowledgment of his silent greeting, then in a daze walked stiffly past him. Where was Drew?

The stranger at the prosecutor's table stood and glanced around the room. "Excuse me," he addressed the group at large. "Which of you is the foreman?"

"I am," Laine responded.

"Ah," he said perfunctorily and walked toward her, extending his hand in a lukewarm handshake. "I'm Warren Elroy, Mr. Kenyon's aide. Sorry to pull a fresh face on you at the last minute, but Mr. Kenyon won't be here today."

Against all reason, Laine's heart sank.

"Regretfully, he was summoned back to Washington very late last evening and he asked me to fill in for him. Mr. Kenyon also asked me to thank the members of the grand jury for their cooperation," Elroy finished.

Laine stared, shaken by the emotional earthquake his words had triggered. But the man before her was blameless. The one responsible for shaking the very foundation of her well-ordered life was far away — out of her reach, but not out of her mind. Andrew Kenyon's substitute stared at her curiously and Laine realized that she had never acknowledged his explanation.

"Thank you, Mr. . . ." She tilted her head, her face still bearing a blank expression.

"Elroy," he provided.

"Yes, sorry. Thank you, Mr. Elroy. I believe we're ready to begin whenever you are."

"Fine. This won't take long. I need to speak to the grand jury about a list of subpoenas to be served." Receiving a nod of agreement from the foreman, he returned to his appointed place.

Laine slumped down in her chair, raised a slender hand, fingertips pressed to her forehead, thumb to cheek, and stroked her furrowed brow as though in deep thought. She hoped the posture hid the tidal wave of tears gathering in her eyes. She wanted to laugh, scream and cry . . . all at the same time. Unable to vent her emotions, she sat perfectly still, not hearing a word as Warren Elroy's voice droned across the room. Laine did the only thing she could do . . . survive the aftermath of Drew Kenyon.

Twenty-four hours later, she was still busy attempting to accomplish that feat when she boarded her flight for Mexico.

50

Chapter 3

"I want out."

"So you've said." John Rankin wondered what the hell had happened to his friend in the two short days he'd been gone from Washington. God, Drew looked awful. In all their association, John had never seen his former top agent so haggard. Several thousand milligrams of vitamins and a twenty-four-hour nap would have done Drew a world of good. "I thought we had this conversation six months ago."

"We did. At the time I was content to go along with your plan to ease out of the department slowly."

"And now?"

"Circumstances have changed."

"What circumstances?" John's eyes narrowed as he watched his friend fidget with the edge of a file folder on his lap.

"Listen, John —"

"No, you listen. In less than six weeks you kiss this department goodbye and all you've got to say is 'Circumstances have changed.' This is your old buddy John you're talking to — a man who's known you longer and probably better than any other human being alive. And all I get are three-word convoluted sentences. You can do better than that, Drew."

"It's personal." He met Rankin's gaze head on. "Very personal."

"What about the case in Dallas?"

"Wakefield and Elroy can handle that standing on their heads." Drew's matter-of-fact rejoinder dismissed the problem.

The rat-a-tat-tat of a yellow pencil against the scarred wooden desk accompanied Rankin's sigh. Drew's special brand of iron-willed determination had often proved an asset in their

51

line of work, but John had no desire to butt heads one-on-one, so he tried the only proven route to success.

"And what about when the deal goes down in San Antonio? You're the only one who can positively ID Barlow. Are you going to let an enemy of the United States of America sell weapons to a Red country and get away with it because you've changed your mind?"

John's predictable maneuver evoked a smile. "Nice try, John, but I've already requested clearance on the videotape of Barlow. Wakefield can watch it until he goes blind. He'll recognize Barlow at fifty paces."

"Well. Seems you've covered all the bases." Rankin knew additional objections would be minor and would be countered with equal finesse . . . except one.

"There's still one last debriefing session, you know."

"Yeah."

A muscle jumped in Drew's rigid neck and it was all the confirmation Rankin needed. Whatever had driven Drew to rush his last days of government service abruptly to a close must be damned important, he decided. Important enough for him to give up the chance to collar a traitor he'd chased since Vietnam. If it were that important, Rankin had to know, both as Drew's friend — and as his boss. Funny, how he still thought of himself as Drew's superior, even after the long months Drew had been with the prosecutor's office. Old habits died hard.

"The only reason I had you dragged into this case in the first place was because of your acquaintance with Barlow. If you've gone over all the material with Wakefield and are satisfied he can do the job, that's good enough for me."

"Thanks, John." Drew's entire body visibly relaxed as though he'd been holding his breath awaiting the outcome of their discussion. The tension immediately returned. "Wait a minute. You've never acceded to a request so fast in all the years I've known you. This was too easy. What gives, John?"

Damn the man's perception, thought Rankin. As usual, Kenyon was right on the money. "Actually, if you hadn't called last night, I would have contacted you. Fact of the matter is, we got word that Barlow's getting antsy, perhaps even suspicious. If your name was ever linked with the operation and Barlow got wind of it . . ." Rankin leaned forward in his swivel chair, resting his forearms on the desk. "I don't need to remind you that he'll kill you if he gets the opportunity, do I?"

"No."

"Still," Rankin said thoughtfully, "a little insurance wouldn't hurt. If I make grumpy noises over the fact you've left early and for good, word should filter through the grapevine quick enough. Just the same, I'd watch my back if I were you. Barlow is positively unbalanced where you're concerned." Rankin's gaze narrowed and his voice lowered. "I've seen men hell-bent for vengeance before, but Barlow's hatred of you is in a class by itself."

"Yeah."

Rankin cleared his throat and looked away. "You need to make yourself scarce for a while anyway. Fortunately, your request fits right into my plan." His tone of voice clearly indicated that had it been otherwise, their conversation would have concluded differently.

"As soon as I've completed my interview with Internal and briefed Wakefield, I'll be gone." Drew glanced at the gruff man on the other side of the desk and knew they would never completely sever connections with each other, no matter where their separate lives might lead. John Rankin had been his teacher, occasional partner and the closest thing to a lifelong friend as he was likely to have.

"Fine. Now, perhaps you'd care to tell me what's so damned urgent you had to get clear early?" Rankin jabbed a finger into the air toward the file folder now resting in Drew's lap.

"I, uh, need to get away."

"If you need a vacation, why didn't you say so? The operation could've been put on hold for a few days. Why the push to terminate?"

"My request has nothing to do with a vacation. I just didn't want to wait any longer to start my 'civilian' life. I've given my country and my government top priority for almost eighteen years and I never have and never will regret it. But my priorities have changed. The kind of assignments you hand out need a man's complete dedication. I can't give you that anymore. Not that what you do isn't important. What I want to do, now, is more important. I have to do this for me. Do you understand?"

"Damn, Drew, that's the longest speech I've ever heard you make. Your 'priority' must be pretty special. I'd like to meet the woman who could get you to change your mind about anything." He smiled at the look of surprise on Kenyon's face. "Don't forget to send me an invitation to the wedding." The smile erupted into a full-blown grin as Drew sputtered the expected denial. "Old buddy, I taught you to read between the lines, remember? Don't try to con the master."

"It's not what you think, John. We haven't . . . I mean, the relationship hasn't progressed . . ."

"Careful, friend, or progress will run right over you. Looks to me like you're already down for the count."

"All right." Drew threw up his hands in good-natured surrender. "I bow before your sage wisdom, not to mention over twenty-five years of marriage."

"Smart kid. Now, get out of here before I change my mind."

Both men rose and shook hands. Drew was genuinely touched by the extra surge of pressure just before John released his grip. He tucked the file under his arm and headed for the door, then stopped and turned back to Rankin.

"Something happens and you get in a bind . . ." He hesitated, then began again. "If you need my testimony, let me know. I can always make time for a brief —" he emphasized the last word "— visit to our nation's capital."

For the two hours and twenty minutes of the flight to Cancún, Laine Stewart did exactly the same thing she'd been doing for the past forty-eight hours — struggled to restore order to her life since discovering that Drew Kenyon had absconded. She propped an elbow on the narrow armrest of her seat and ran her fingertips across her brow. Lord, she made him sound like a thief, looting and then stealing away in the dead of night. But hadn't he done just that? Hadn't he stolen something valuable — her peace of mind — then fled?

Oh, stop being so melodramatic! He didn't take anything; only accepted what she had so willingly offered. And besides, what was so earth-shattering about a simple kiss between two consenting adults? *Simple!* If you called a mind-jarring temptation's kiss "simple." *Just because the earth moved under your feet doesn't mean he felt the same tremor.*

But he had, something deep inside insisted; he'd experienced the very same excitement. What she had seen in Drew's eyes, felt in his touch, tasted on his lips, was impossible to fake. *For crying out loud, Laine, you're driving yourself mad!*

But she couldn't stop. The scene of their last few minutes together played over and over like a mental video recorder, reaching the same conclusion each time. Regardless of what Drew had said, he was strong; stronger than she could ever hope to be. He had known the situation between them was impossible, so he'd simply removed himself from temptation. Yes, Drew had wanted her — that much was abundantly clear — but not at the cost of his career. Laine and Drew had stood at a crossroads in that darkened parking lot and his vision had been much clearer than hers. Laine knew in her head that the decision he had made was the right one, yet her heart beat faster over the memory of one sweet, wild kiss.

With a sigh, she peered out the small window of the chartered jet and watched the jungles of the Yucatán peninsula rising to meet her. The hectic schedule of the next few days would help shove thoughts of Drew Kenyon to the far corners of her mind; Laine welcomed the distraction.

The tropical sun beat down relentlessly upon the disembarking passengers and, coupled with the high humidity, clothes and hairdos immediately went limp. The unair-conditioned terminal provided no relief; fortunately Laine's flight had been the first arrival of the morning, leaving the airport uncrowded. Other flights, though, began landing rapidly thereafter and the terminal was soon deluged with perspiring tourists. Since the level of noise rose swiftly to an irritating pitch, Laine was grateful that the customary luggage inspection was only cursory.

Bags in hand, she waited rather impatiently at the end of a long line of travelers seeking a cab. In the interim, she inspected the throng of tourists, noting how fast the mass of human bodies had moved through immigration, customs and on to the luggage retrieval area. Surprisingly, the entire process appeared to flow quite well in spite of the numerous incoming flights. All of this was grist for Laine's own mill — storing and processing data for future reference.

She mentally saluted the airport personnel and hoped devoutly that nothing disturbed the Mexican economy between then and convention time. With six hundred conventioneers expected, chaos would reign and the meeting would launch on a sour note if her people flew in to find they must fight their way through immigration, then wait half an hour for luggage to clear. A check appeared in the "approved" column of the lengthy list Laine carried in her head. Laine prepared to raise her arm in the universal cab-hailing gesture when all at once she felt compelled to turn once more and scan the crowded terminal.

He stood among the throng, his back to her. Laine's eyes widened with disbelief. The man looked like . . . no . . . couldn't be. Still, the shoulders were broad, the hair was the right shade of blond. Laine held her breath, a smile of welcome waiting in the wings of her heart, as the man turned, smiled and waved at someone. His smile was beautiful, but it wasn't for her.

He wasn't Drew! Breath sighed from Laine's body in a steady stream; she didn't know whether from relief or disappointment. Although the man was good-looking, he was not Drew. So much for putting Drew Kenyon to the far corners of her mind. Discontented and frustrated, she almost snapped the head off the first cabbie who came near her.

After checking into the Plaza Americana hotel, Laine confirmed her appointments for the next day. Satisfied with the schedule, she unpacked and changed into walking shorts and a safari shirt. Hours of the longed-for free time stretched before her, but the actuality didn't thrill her as she had expected. To her dismay, Laine discovered that she felt unsettled and tense. Determined to relax, she stepped out onto her private patio. Settling herself on the comfortable lounger she opened the novel she'd selected at the airport book stand.

The cover proclaimed it to be a sweeping saga of romance and adventure while displaying the two main characters in a torrid embrace. The heroine appeared to be in danger of catching a chest cold and the hero's attention seemed to be directed to that area of concern. Examining the scene closely, she couldn't for the life of her think why the standard historical-romance cover had first caught her attention. The woman was a ravishing creature, her head thrown back to expose a slender throat and a mane of thick blond hair. The hero was tall, broad shouldered and equally blond. And he had striking blue eyes.

By the time she reached page forty and couldn't remember a word written on pages one through thirty-nine, she decided to give it up. Unusually distracted and irritated at herself for allowing the distraction to bloom into restlessness, Laine stared out toward the beach. Her unvarnished nails idly tapped the bared chest of the male on the slick book cover while random thoughts of another, extremely three-dimensional man plagued her.

The novel hit the cushion of the lounger with a loud whack and five minutes later, camera in hand, she was on her way into Cancún City. She spent the remainder of the day playing tourist, browsing in the bustling market and bargaining with the merchants. By the time she returned to the hotel around sundown she was hot, tired . . . and still restless. After a shower and a dinner she barely remembered, Laine wandered along the beach, still seeking a sedative for her restive spirit.

Slowly, the continuous ebb and flow of the tide as it washed over the sand and hissed against the rocks lulled her into a quiet, reflective mood. She found herself evaluating the past year of her life from a very critical viewpoint, and in doing so was forced to face the reason for her soul-searching.

Since the moment she'd looked up into a certain pair of incredible blue eyes, her life hadn't been the same. *She* hadn't been the same. Was it possible for one man to disrupt her orderly existence so completely? Yes, if that one man was Drew Kenyon.

Why? He loosely fit the category of personable, rising young executive type she had been seeing since her divorce. Though small in number, her escorts had always been very bright, self-confident, career-oriented men with a strong sense of what it took to compete in the world around them. As a matter of fact, they were usually more interested in their careers than in anything else. So why did Drew Kenyon affect her in a way no man ever had?

Because he made her *feel*. Not just sexually — though that was definitely part of it — but he elicited emotions in her that she had tried to suppress for so long: loneliness, passion and tenderness — all the feelings connected to her image of herself as a woman. How long since she'd felt the urge to press her body next to a man's and revel in the knowledge that he wanted her? When was the last time she had felt the sweet, slow burn of desire? Now, along comes a man she can't possibly have and her pulse rate and good sense go sky-high. If one kiss could turn her to steaming liquid, what would making love with him be like? The thought jarred Laine out of her reverie, bringing the smell of the ocean and the feel of the water over her bare feet sharply into awareness.

Night had fallen and a full moon shone like a magnificent pearl against indigo velvet. Laine was shocked to see how far she had come from the sandy cove of her hotel. The beach was almost deserted and a sudden uneasiness crept over her. She glanced around and was relieved to notice a young couple sitting on a blanket not far away and a man strolling up the beach toward her. As she started back, the man stopped, stared at her for a long moment, then changed directions and crossed the sand at a right angle to her position. As he passed under a high-intensity light, he glanced quickly over his shoulder and Laine caught a glimpse of a darkly tanned face and a black mustache. Grateful that the swarthy stranger had not crossed her path, she hurried back to the hotel.

That night she slept soundly. Only her unconscious refused to accept the command to push thoughts of Drew Kenyon aside, as her dreams were filled with images of a disturbingly handsome, blond man who smiled and made exquisite love to her. Well, nobody could control their dreams, could they?

The following morning the staff at the Plaza Americana was friendly, efficient and amicable. Laine's meetings produced quick decisions and by midafternoon all details had been deftly catalogued and the management staff duly thanked. She was content, knowing the intricate plans would go off as well as possible in February when the first conventioneers arrived. Her business in Cancún was nearing completion, with the exception of checking out the side tours to be offered for the group.

Practically in the amount of time it takes to say "Last one in the water . . ." Laine was enjoying a relaxing swim. Then, basking on a contoured vinyl recliner beneath the glorious Cancún sun, she wiggled down contentedly to people-watch through half-closed eyelids.

Inhaling deeply, her lungs filled with the exhilarating sea air. Her damp black maillot clung to her body, causing her skin to tingle deliciously as the ocean breeze drifted across exposed flesh, where a salt residue shimmered on her bare arms and legs, leaving a pearlescent sheen. Laine glanced down at her out-stretched body and silently approved — not bad for almost thirty. She sighed and turned her attention to two small children shrieking and dancing in the rolling waves.

Sunshine glinted blindingly off the white sand, forcing Laine to raise her hand to shade her view in spite of her designer sunglasses. A man and a woman joined the children, obviously the parents, by the way they were greeted. Nice family, Laine thought. The mother's petite blondness foretold the future appearance of the little girl beside her — a duplicate in miniature. The son, likewise reflective of the father's coloring, was promoting, without much success, a game of keep away.

The man was attractive, but not as good-looking as . . . *Oh damn!* Disturbing thoughts of Drew Kenyon appeared like magic. *You fool! Why do you want to ruin a perfectly beautiful day?*

But some thoughts, once bidden, are twice as determined to remain. And so, no matter how hard Laine tried to force mental images of Drew from her mind, the vision would not budge. Her hazel eyes unconsciously scanned the male occupants on the beach and in the water — appraising them, comparing them to the one who was incomparable. Laine's fruitless observation continued until her gaze fell on a superb specimen knifing his way through the water toward the beach. Powerful shoulders and arms rhythmically moved him effortlessly through the Caribbean, his water-darkened head rotating smoothly with each stroke.

The swimmer slowed, then stood in chest-high water. Mesmerized, Laine was whisked unwittingly back into her juryroom fantasy. Watching the swimmer push his body through the swirling surf, she imagined she saw not a stranger, but the man of her dreams.

Nearer and nearer he came, saltwater sluicing down a magnificently proportioned body, sunlight glistening on his golden head, wet swim trunks molding trim hips. The muscles in his thighs flexed with each step and Laine could not take her eyes from the embodiment of her fantasy.

Heart racing like the wind, chest heaving with the effort to gulp precious air, Laine fought the waves of tremors engulfing her entire body.

Nearer, nearer still, her fantasy advanced, until the phantom stopped beside her. Slowly, he dropped to the sand next to her. Entranced, she watched a bead of water begin to trickle slowly down his cheek toward his sensual mouth. Hopelessly continuing to live out the dream her hand moved to interrupt and capture the droplet.

In the space of time alloted between heartbeats, fantasy became reality.

"I told you . . . I couldn't let you walk away from me," said a heart-stopping, vividly remembered, all-too-real voice.

Chapter 4

Laine blinked, then jerked her hand back as if she'd been burned. "You're not supposed . . . how did . . . you followed me!" she sputtered.

"It's a public beach. I saw you sitting here and decided that was all the recommendation I needed." He smiled that damnably charming smile. Laine didn't miss the wordplay, but before she could check herself, anger exploded to cover her shock.

"There is no way this could be considered a chance encounter. Not in the span of two lifetimes — much less two days!"

He started to speak, but she cut him off. "And don't come back with that nonsense about circumstantial evidence."

"I was just about to say, what a coincidence."

"Don't." She threw the word over her shoulder as she leaned across the lounger and hurriedly collected her beach paraphernalia. Instantly, his body shifted and strong fingers locked around her wrists.

"Laine?" She tugged against his hold. "Did I scare you?"

"Of course you did." She snapped her head around.

"Didn't you recognize me?"

"Yes, but I didn't know you were real!"

"Didn't know I was . . ." He looked at her oddly. "Did you think I was a figment of your imagination?" He chuckled.

Confusion warred with embarrassment as her eyes widened and her cheeks flamed. She averted her gaze. He was here but he wasn't supposed to be. She wanted him here, but she shouldn't. None of this made any sense. "You followed me," she reiterated, her voice raspy.

"Yes."

"But why?"

"Laine, look at me." He placed a finger beneath her chin and tilted her head upward. Drew stared into the bewildered face of the woman he had not been able to put from his mind since the first time he saw her. How was she going to react to what he was about to say? For once in his life, he fervently hoped the truth would *not* set him free.

"Have you ever been lonely?"

Stunned at his question, she merely nodded.

"The night we kissed —" He stopped, then the strength of his convictions took hold and his voice became eloquently potent. "That night after you drove away, I was out of my mind with loneliness and I couldn't figure out why. Then I realized that it only seemed worse because for a few minutes I'd held you in my arms, then you were gone. So, yes, I followed you. I had to." He smiled his well-remembered little-boy smile and, despite growing misgivings, Laine's heart melted. "God knows, I never expected it, but whatever's between us is so rare, we'd be fools to turn our backs on it."

"But . . . we have to. It's unethical, maybe even illegal for us to . . . to be together."

"Not any more. The Reese case, or any other grand-jury case, no longer stands between us."

"I don't understand."

"I made the decision months ago to leave the department. I turned the Dallas presentation over to another prosecutor and decided to leave earlier than I'd planned." A smile played at the corners of his lips. "Isn't it nice that we both like tropical vacations?"

"Just like that?"

"Just like that. Don't you believe me?"

"I'd like to . . ." Her voice trailed off to the barest whisper. "But?"

"But, I'm not sure it will work."

"Neither am I. But I'm certain we have more going for us than the obvious. I want to give us a chance, but I'm not interested in a one-sided relationship. Tell me you don't feel the same way and I'll walk off this beach and never bother you again. Tell me to go and I will."

"I can't. I mean, I don't know if I want you to go . . . or stay," she said honestly.

"What would it take for you to know?"

"Time and —" She looked away, unable to believe what she was saying, much less what she was contemplating. Her head hurt from confusion. Was he talking about an affair? Was she seriously considering it if he were?

"Is there something else?"

"Drew —" she met his gaze directly "— I need stability."

For a moment, he said nothing. Then his eyes closed briefly before he spoke. "Are you talking about the stability of knowing you are loved, or of promises of forever?"

"I'm talking about one man and one woman, a family, a home. No living on the wild side or seeking the thrill-a-minute existence. I've had enough of that kind of man to last me a lifetime. I'm talking about permanence, Drew. Plain ole everyday permanence, nothing less."

"And you're not sure I'm the permanent type, is that it?"

She lowered her gaze and nervously ran a fingernail in a figure-eight pattern in the sand. "Something like that."

"You're wrong, Laine. I want the same thing everyone wants: to love and be loved. Up until now I haven't had the opportunity to do much of either."

She studied his face and watched his eyes, searching for some sign that he spoke from the heart, but he looked down.

"Well," he said matter-of-factly, "all I can offer you with any certainty is the time." Then he lifted his head and grinned.

"Shall we begin with dinner around seven tonight?"

"Are you sure?"

"About dinner? I'll say. Lunch on the flight was —"

"I'm not talking about food and you know it." She gave a poor imitation of an exasperated scowl.

"Every step up that beach was pure agony. I was scared to death you would turn me down flat. But the way you looked at me, watched me, made me certain of one thing: whether consciously or not, you had been remembering me the same way I had been remembering you."

"I . . . I thought you were another daydream," Laine confessed falteringly.

"Did you?" Outlandishly elated at her words, he leaned forward and gently placed his lips at the very tip of her earlobe. "I can't count the times I've dreamed of you, day and night."

Laine's arms slid comfortably around his shoulders; her fingers unerringly found their way into the damp curls lying against the back of his neck.

Eyes closed, Drew released a deep sigh. Never in his life had he desired a woman the way he wanted Laine. He trembled with the need to have her lie next to him, cry out her need for him, pour over him the sweetness only she possessed. Drew was a nanosecond away from kissing her in a way guaranteed to embarrass them both. Too fast, he cautioned himself. If he pushed her he would regret it. He wasn't just after a couple of nights under a tropical moon; the union of spirits as well as bodies was his ultimate goal. Meanwhile her skin, soft and warm against his, drove all "spiritual" thoughts from his head. She felt so good and he wanted her so badly.

"I think . . . I think we've got to get off this beach before I make a complete ass of myself in public, is what I think." Hastily he drew Laine to her feet. "Come on, I'll walk you upstairs."

A few moments later, outside her second-floor room, Laine suddenly turned to Drew. "Where are you staying?"

"Fourth floor." He pumped the air with his thumb.

"I see." An unmistakable spark of anger flashed in hazel eyes.

"What you don't see," Drew stated in a tightly controlled voice, "is me, edging my way inside your door. And you won't, unless I'm invited." His azure gaze drilled her. "I won't lie and say I don't want to make love to you until you beg me to stop. That's not my style. You asked for time and I agreed. But you have to know how much I want you."

"I don't . . ."

"I can wait," he said softly. "Just don't get the idea that I'm made of cast iron. I'm not." He cupped her face in his hands. With the lightest of strokes his thumbs caressed the soft fullness of her bottom lip, then slowly he lowered his mouth to hers.

The kiss was everything she remembered. And more.

Deliciously warm and infinitely resourceful, his tongue coaxed, tasted, stroked the inner softness of her mouth. She strained to eliminate the scant air-space between, arching her back in silent demand. Eager arms snaked around Drew's shoulders, but still she wasn't close enough. Need answered need. With relentless determination he deepened the kiss until pinpricks of light danced behind Laine's eyelids and her whole body felt lighter than air. His tongue did mind-bending things to the inside of her mouth and she moaned, compelled to chase its slow withdrawal as he reluctantly ended the kiss.

"Laine, Laine, Laine," he whispered hoarsely on an indrawn breath, bringing his forehead to rest against hers. Strong hands trembled as they caressed her shoulders. His body was on fire with the need to feel her warm and willing beneath him. If he didn't get the hell away from her right this minute . . .

67

Reluctantly he withdrew, pried the room key from her white-knuckled grip, unlocked the door and gently but firmly pushed her inside.

"Seven o'clock in the lobby." His voice was whisky rough with desire as he turned and walked away.

Laine heard the door to her room close behind her, but didn't remember stepping inside. Unconsciously, her right index fingertip touched her swollen bottom lip and slid from side to side. The movement halted; she jerked her hand away from her hot skin and stared wide-eyed at the fingertip. "Oh my God!" she whispered.

Trembling, she wobbled to the bed and dropped to the mattress. Whatever possessed her! She clutched her midsection in a futile attempt to still the raging turmoil inside. The kiss had affected her far more than she'd intended. Far more than she was prepared to handle. The inside of her mouth still tingled from his plundering tongue. "Oh my God," she intoned. He was no longer just a fantasy, but flesh and blood. And he was here, telling her he wanted her, asking for her to want him. Want him? She wanted him so much it hurt. Dear Lord, how was she going to withstand the sensual bombardment of Drew Kenyon? Better yet, how was she going to combat her urge to surrender?

Memories of her disastrous marriage were still vivid enough to make her more than just a little cautious about another relationship. True, at some point in the future, if the right man came along, marriage might be a possibility. But what if Drew was the right man? He couldn't be, she reminded herself. Even though the barrier of their positions on the grand jury no longer existed, the question of their life values remained. Was he the Rock of Gibraltar, or a rolling stone? Only time would provide the answer. The condition she'd asked for had been granted. Why had she even made such a dangerous request? Why hadn't she given him a simple "no." The truth was she couldn't because her feelings for Drew weren't simple. They were complicated and confusing. She sighed, realizing full well she was already hip-deep in a situation bounded on all sides by her own rules.

A short time later, refreshed and ready to face Drew, Laine tapped her sandaled toes on the marble-tiled lobby floor. She checked her watch. Five minutes after seven. Maybe he wasn't coming. Maybe he'd had second thoughts. She turned toward the breezeway connecting the main part of the hotel lobby to the guest rooms and a hot, almost violent rush of relentless desire raced through her veins the instant she caught sight of him. Until that very moment, she had convinced herself she could hold her own against the power of this man. Watching him stride toward her, she knew she was lost. He was undoubtedly the most attractive man she had ever laid eyes on.

Her gaze followed the neat crease in his navy slacks up to the narrow waist, then farther to the wide chest covered with a green and blue striped polo shirt. Her body was acutely, disturbingly attuned to the movement of his every muscle. He was so damned sexy!

From across the lobby, his twilight-blue gaze locked with her gold-flecked hazel one. Each step across the tiled floor brought him closer to the vision who had stolen his breath away the moment he saw her. Their gazes remained locked as Drew closed the distance between them. Automatically, his hand sought hers.

"Hungry?" he inquired in a hushed tone.

"Starved," came her equally hushed response.

"Me, too."

"Where?"

"Where?" he echoed.

"Dinner. Where are we having dinner?"

Drew blinked. "Yes, we have to eat dinner. Where?"

"Where?"

"There's an echo in here," he elucidated teasingly, shaking off the remaining wisps of sensual fog. He smiled, wishing he never had to be any farther from her than he was at this moment. "Ever been to Carlos and Charlie's?" he asked in a tone of voice that made Laine regret she'd never been to many places with him.

She shook her head, returning his smile.

"A must — lots of local color — you'll love it."

As they moved toward the door, Drew slipped a hand to the small of her back, only to discover he was touching exactly that — the small of her very naked back! The sundress she wore was daringly cut to the waist and Drew almost bit a hole in his lower lip trying to hold back a groan. *I'll never live to see the sun rise. I'll die of frustration long before then.* He cast a discerning eye to the front of the dress, which confirmed his prediction. The lightweight cotton fabric molded her breasts and midriff so enticingly, his imagination began working overtime. The color matched the blue of the Caribbean and enhanced the newly acquired golden glow of her skin. Drew released her waist in favor of grasping her less-arousing, slender hand.

"Taxi? Or are you game to try Cancún's idea of mass transit?" He admired the way the blue cotton hugged her breasts as she breathed.

"Oh, let's throw caution to the winds and act like tourists," Laine decided. "The last time I was here, I hit the jackpot and wound up sitting near to a small boy holding two chickens. No telling what tonight's trip may hold."

No telling, Drew silently echoed, just as a man came through the hotel doors and nearly collided with Laine. The white-suited stranger mumbled an accented apology and tipped his straw hat, but kept his head bent. Drew glanced over his shoulder as he escorted Laine over the cobblestone walkway leading to the bus stop. After years of depending on his instincts, a cultivated sixth sense provided an inner alert system that seldom failed him. At the moment it was clanging like a call for a three-alarm fire. For some reason the man hadn't wanted Drew or Laine to see his face. Drew knew it just as he knew the sun would come up the next morning. There was more to the stranger than met the eye. He fought the need for a second look and told himself that his reaction had been out of habit. Wasn't that the very thing he was trying to put behind him? He was so accustomed to strangers in strange places, instinct overruled reason. He would have to watch himself or Laine would think he was paranoid.

The bus ground to a halt as they approached the bus stop and shortly thereafter they were abruptly deposited in front of Carlos and Charlie's Restaurant, the stranger forgotten. Dinner in the quaint beachfront setting was delicious . . . and quiet. They each seemed satisfied simply to be together, enjoying each other's company.

Their ride back to the hotel, however, was a complete about-face — fast and furious. The bus drivers in Cancún were not known for their restraint behind the wheel. Laine swore that the driver deliberately hit every pothole and rock in the road as she was repeatedly bumped and jostled on the narrow bench seat, bringing her into constant contact with Drew's lean frame. Each time they touched, Laine felt she had been branded with a white-hot poker. By the time they stepped off the dubious mode of transportation, her whole body felt as if it had been electrically charged with multiple volts of Drew Kenyon, and her senses were on the verge of blowing a fuse.

When Drew captured her hand as they strolled across the

lobby, she felt her high-voltage indicator jump into the danger zone. This sort of atmosphere was not going to promote getting to know each other except in the biblical sense. She was determined to keep her emotions in check when Drew suggested they have a drink by the pool.

"It's too pleasant outside to go back into a stuffy room." His voice soothed and persuaded her. "Besides," he added with a sheepish grin, "I don't imagine I'll get much sleep tonight anyway."

"All right." She agreed to both the drink and the improbability of sleep.

Drinks in hand a few minutes later, they seated themselves on comfortable lounge chairs beside the shimmering water as silence and a balmy breeze wafted over them.

"Laine —"

"Drew —"

"You first," he offered.

"I've been thinking." The quiver in her soft voice matched the trembling in her hand as it held the cool glass.

"About my unexpected appearance, or your reaction?"

"Both." Nervously, she twirled the straw in her drink while her thoughts raced ahead, trying to form the right words.

"I thought you made everything crystal clear this afternoon. We play by your rules, or we don't play."

"That's oversimplified and a little harsh, don't you think?"

"I sounded bitter, didn't I? Sorry. I may chafe a bit under the restrictions, but don't worry, I'll adjust. I'm not used to playing by anyone's rules but my own." He smiled, but she had the feeling he should have tagged "and win" to the statement.

"That's exactly what I've been thinking about, Drew. You go your own way, without answering to anyone. Won't you come to regret you resigned, possibly before you really wanted to, just to pursue a relationship that may not work out?"

"Laine, the fact that I resigned as federal prosecutor had nothing to do with you. I would have left even if I'd never met you. Do you understand? I don't want you to blame yourself in any way. The decision was mine and made long before I came to Dallas."

Laine stared at him, wanting desperately to believe, but afraid to. And what happens when we leave here? she wanted to ask. What becomes of a tropical affair when the cold winds of logic and home sweep in?

He reached over to her and stroked a dark curl sensuously between his thumb and index finger. "Does that answer most of your questions?"

"Yes," she lied, loving the way even his slightest touch made her body vibrate right down to her toes. Her heart was fluttering in her breast like a hummingbird's wings. "Everything is happening so fast —"

"But it feels right. You can't deny the way you feel when we're together any more than I can."

Simple, straightforward logic — the same kind Laine had used to convince herself an affair with Drew was impossible — now worked against her. Her reasoning was ineffectual when it came to answering the last question. Every time she looked into those striking blue eyes of his, reason seemed to abandon her, leaving pure instinct in its place. And operating on instinct alone, her body, if not her mind, never failed to respond to him. Even now, she found herself drowning in crystal-blue pools darkened to indigo, desire flashing from their depths.

"We both know this is special. Give us some time, sweetheart. Give me time to show you the kind of magic we can make together." His gaze searched her face, reaching into her thoughts.

"Time may make the magic disappear," she said, hoping for a convincing protest. How soon had the magic gone in her marriage?

"Not the kind we'll make." His voice, smooth and thick as rich cream, flowed over her.

What defense was there against the potent brand of ammunition Drew used with such deadly accuracy? She surrendered. Laine breathed an acquiescing sigh as their lips met in a tender but all-too-brief kiss. She shivered when he withdrew his moist, warm mouth.

"Cold?" His quiet concern only deepened the spell he had cast over her.

"Not when you kiss me like you do."

"Then I'll just have to keep it up, won't I?"

An imperceptible nod of her head was all she could trust herself to give in answer.

The poolside area had begun to fill slowly with people. Other couples, lovers, strolled arm in arm. Moonlight, soft music and a tropical night worked its spell on everyone. All too soon, they were two among many.

"Time to go inside," Drew insisted as he hauled himself from the lounger, then extended a hand for her. "We have all day tomorrow to relax and enjoy each other."

"Tomorrow! Oh, no-o-o!" Laine exclaimed, for the first time even thinking beyond the present.

"No?" Drew echoed, alarmed.

"I forgot," Laine almost wailed, "I've one more tour in the morning. Damn, damn, damn."

"How long will the tour take?"

Laine frowned and looked at him beseechingly. "Almost all day," she said with exasperation. "It goes to the Mayan ruins at Tulum, then a stop at some place called Xel-Há." Her tone was almost apologetic. "I'm sorry, I wish . . ."

"You'll love it." Resignation underscored each word. "Tulum is one of the most beautiful spots on the Yucatán."

"You've been there?" Laine asked, a germ of an idea taking root.

"Uh-hmm."

"Would . . . would it bore you to go again?"

"Not if I'm with you. What time does the bus leave?"

Laine cast him a dubious glance. "Uh . . . eight-thirty. If that's too early, I'll understand perf—"

"I'd love to go with you," Drew hastened to interrupt. "How about meeting me for breakfast an hour before? If seven-thirty's not too early for you?"

"No, no, breakfast is fine." Losing a few minutes of sleep was no sacrifice compared to time spent with Drew. In fact, losing sleep over Drew Kenyon was becoming a way of life. By tacit consent, they slowly strolled arm in arm; the tropical night breezes wafted around them, creating a soft cocoon of intimacy. At the door to Laine's room, Drew turned to face her. Laine held her breath expectantly.

"Wear your bathing suit." He dropped the suggestion with understated nonchalance. His voice, deep and sensual, sent a ripple of renewed awareness through her.

"I beg your pardon?"

"Wear shorts over your swimsuit tomorrow," he clarified, smiling broadly at her reaction. "Tulum will be sweltering. By the time we reach Xel-Há, believe me, you'll be ready for a cool dip. The lagoon there is beautiful. You can swim right alongside the fish," he promised.

"Sounds heavenly."

"It is," Drew assured urbanely, thinking some heavenly thoughts about her.

Polite conversation faltered as silence settled around them. Without realizing it, Laine retreated until her shoulders and

75

buttocks touched the wooden door. Talk about backing yourself into a corner! she thought, feeling awkward, almost shy, and certainly at a loss for words. She was scared he would kiss her and terrified he wouldn't. She needn't have worried.

"I promised you could set the pace. And just to show you I'm a man of my word, I want you to know exactly what I intend to do," Drew said in his best prosecutor instructing jury voice. "I'm going to give you a lingering, passionate kiss — enough to last me through a long night — then get the hell to my room."

With palms flat against the door on either side of her head, Drew leaned forward. Touching her nowhere except on her mouth, he acted out his narration. The kiss was long and oh-so-sweet, his tongue dipping repeatedly in quick, hot forays to collect the nectar of her mouth. Then the kiss ended, and when she opened her eyes he was gone.

Laine sank her teeth into her bottom lip to keep from calling him back. Drew stepped into the waiting elevator and turned to face her down the length of the hallway.

"Sweet dreams," he called softly, before the elevator doors swooshed closed and he disappeared from sight.

Chapter 5

Drew was leaning against the railing of the breeze-way the next morning when Laine stepped off the elevator. Navy shorts, piped in red, positively worshiped his trim hips and muscular thighs. Epaulets, secured with brass buttons, rested at the shoulders of the matching navy and red polo shirt. Laine promptly decided that if his clothing was the uniform of the day, she was ready to enlist. One elbow and hip were propped against the banister, one leg crossed over the other at the ankles in a devil-may-care posture. The breeze from the Caribbean feathered his blond hair, adding to the rakish pose.

Sinfully handsome, she thought, the sight of him so disturbing she felt light-headed. She marveled at how his body conveyed such forceful masculinity while looking so smooth, sleek and relaxed. Drew Kenyon reminded her of a magnificent race car she had once seen in a photograph — bold, striking, elegantly powerful — the Ferrari of the male species. Then he saw her and straightened as she headed toward him. Her heart was pounding in her chest, pulse rate elevating with every step she took.

"Good morning," Drew greeted, wishing the words were being spoken across a pillow instead of a public breezeway.

"Good morning." Unknowingly, Laine's wishes paralleled his.

Neither asked how the other had slept — it was a moot point, under the circumstances. Instead, they filled their senses with the sight and smell of each other.

Laine's gaze roamed lovingly over his face, noting the more pronounced creases bracketing his mouth. The aroma of soap, shaving cream, and cologne mingled to throw a hammerlock on her senses. Her heart was still trying to outpace Secretariat as she placed a hand over the spot to calm its thundering.

Drew's gaze glided ravenously over her features, noting the faint smudges beneath her eyes. A whiff of her memorable perfume rose to tantalize his nostrils. He slowly imbibed the fragrance, relishing the scent that was uniquely Laine.

Facing each other, they stood for several minutes in total mutual absorption, until each was thoroughly saturated. Then and only then did they turn, without speaking or touching, to make their way into the dining room.

Laine couldn't remember a time when food tasted so good. The pungent smell of fresh-brewed coffee, tangy fruit and hot bread, mixed with the already tantalizing aroma of Drew, charged all her sensory nerves. She felt, tasted and smelled the world as if for the first time — a dizzying experience. By the end of the meal she was functioning on automatic pilot, trying to stay afloat in an ocean of sensations.

Drew watched the vivid excitement sparkle in her eyes, knowing exactly what she was feeling. He was with her every step of the way — treading water in the whirlpool of mutual susceptibility. By the time they walked into the bright morning sunshine, Drew was apprehensive about the day. He wasn't sure he could keep from hauling her off into the jungle at the first opportunity. But as they boarded the bus, thoughts of passion were quickly shoved to one side as his internal warning system jumped to full alert.

The man who had collided with them as they exited the hotel the night before was sitting on the last seat at the back.

Drew was certain it was the same man and just as certain that his presence on the bus was not coincidental. Instinctively he drew closer to Laine as they moved down the aisle of the bus. Glancing over his shoulder at the position of the driver's rearview mirror, he calculated angles and vantage points. Laine was about to slide across the seat to sit next to the window when he placed a hand on her shoulder.

"Would you mind if we switch seats? Sometimes I get a little claustrophobic. Don't worry," he added with a grin. "I promise not to obscure your view."

Drew looked into the driver's mirror and evaluated what he saw. *Jet-black hair, mustache, darkly tanned, about thirty. Nothing out of the ordinary. But then, ordinary people made the best watchers.* Was the man following him, or had the protective paranoia he valued for years gone a little haywire? For his own satisfaction, Drew decided to make a point of inspecting the man at close range as soon as possible, and without Laine's knowledge. Meanwhile, he knew right where the stranger was.

The air inside the bus corresponded to the rising temperature outside, becoming cloyingly heavy. Strategically placed small fans whirled above the heads of the passengers, but the blades only served to stir the stifling air without reducing the temperature. Laine was becoming increasingly uncomfortable, a discomfort stemming not so much from the lack of cool air as from the sensual fever radiating between her body and Drew's.

Shoulder to shoulder, hip to hip on the narrow bench seat, nothing separated them except their imaginations. Laine cast a sidelong glance at Drew as the bus pulled away from the hotel. She sensed a tension in him that had not been present at breakfast. He was gazing out the window; his left hand absently worried the armrest of the seat, but she got the feeling his mind was far removed from the passing countryside. Sitting "cheek to cheek," as it were, obviously didn't seem to affect him the same way it did her.

Drew felt Laine's intense study and cautioned himself not to let his suspicions put a damper on their day. He turned to her, his face relaxing into a devastating smile. "Did I tell you how beautiful you look today?"

"I . . . no. Thank you," she said, a little surprised by the mood change.

"N-i-i-ce bathing suit." His gaze dropped from her eyes to the revealing neckline of her maillot. "I liked the one you wore yesterday, too." He reached out and ran an index finger from the side of her throat, over her shoulder, down the inside of her arm. "Particularly the way it was cut up high on your hips and low across your breasts."

Laine's lips parted and she glanced away. He would drive her crazy with such talk. "Has anyone ever told you how disarming you can be?"

"Is that what I do — disarm you?"

"You know you do," she said a little breathlessly.

"All right —" he raised his hands in mock surrender "— I'll behave myself."

For the rest of the trip he was as good as his word and it very nearly drove Laine crazy. Bogged down in the quagmire of her emotions, she continued to waver between wanting him to pay attention to her and being uncomfortable when he did. Her difficulty was magnified by the close quarters of the bus. Seated beside her, his every movement telegraphed through his body to hers. Everything about him was seductive: his clean smell, his tanned, muscular thighs, even the smooth sound of his voice as they made casual conversation.

At least Laine hoped her half of the conversation sounded casual. God knows, she was trying like hell to make it appear that way. Success was doubtful.

The bus swayed almost continually, causing their bodies to brush against each other. More than once, the little finger of Drew's right hand grazed her kneecap. Laine squirmed in her seat. Being next to him, touching, yet not really touching, was torture — pure, unadulterated, sublime torture.

Determined to direct her mind away from its erotic wander-

80

ing, Laine concentrated on watching the landscape. Having taken the aisle seat, she was forced to look across Drew to view the scenery. The road cut through the jungle, a dove-colored ribbon across green velvet. Lush foliage rose on either side to flank the edges like reed soldiers at attention. Occasional splashes of color flashed out of the green background as brightly hued tropical flowers and birds appeared. A brilliant splotch of red several hundred yards ahead unexpectedly caught Laine's eye.

"Look!" she exclaimed, rolling onto her hip and stretching her torso across Drew's immediately rigid body. Without thinking, she simultaneously braced her left hand on Drew's bare thigh to point toward the breathtaking sight of a gigantic tree covered in glorious red-orange blossoms.

"Oh-h-h, how fantastic!" Laine proclaimed. "The color, it's . . ." her excited voice trailed off as her head turned toward Drew and she discovered their noses were only inches apart ". . . ab-so-lute-ly . . ." she finished breathlessly ". . . fantastic." The last word was barely audible.

Blue eyes, darkened to the color of pewter, stared in disbelief at the stunned expression on Laine's face. Drew struggled unsuccessfully to keep his own expression unreadable in view of the fact that his reaction translated a bit more obviously than hers. Laine's enticing body draped across his made coherent thought very difficult.

Drew was on the verge of shifting away from the pressure of her warm hand when the bus struck a king-size bump.

Laine's left arm buckled, pitching her across his lap. He caught her and in the process their bodies tangled intimately. She found herself half sitting on him, nearly chest to chest. One of her hands rested several inches beneath the hem of his shorts. For one distressing second, Drew and Laine froze.

Very quickly Laine twisted against his hard body sliding her knee across his unyielding thigh in an innocently seductive gesture.

Drew clenched his teeth and struggled to control his arousal. How the hell did he expect to convince her his feelings went beyond sex if he couldn't exercise a little self-control? *A little self-control!* Tons, not ounces of restraint were needed for this situation. Watching her through lowered lashes, he noted the delicate touch of pink suffusing her cheek and the sheen of perspiration on her upper lip. God, but he wanted to kiss her. Right here. Right now. His head lifted from the back of the seat before he checked himself.

Trembling with embarrassment, Laine was enormously grateful that the tour guide picked that moment to begin lecturing to the travelers.

"As you see, Yucatán is very colorful," the guide, Raphael, offered in somewhat broken English. "Much beautiful flowers and trees. Like Flamboiana." He gestured as another splotch of bright red whizzed past. Oohs and ahs floated through the interior of the bus as all the passengers except two turned to admire the tree bearing the gloriously colored blossoms. "Flamboiana. It means —" Raphael hesitated "— royal oinciana. Very pretty. All tourists say the same." He smiled proudly.

Laine's forced concentration was suddenly demolished as a deep voice beside her confirmed, "Fantastic. Absolutely fantastic."

Laine turned to face Drew, half surprised, half uncertain at the seductively teasing tone of the first words he'd spoken since her ill-fated sprawl. He was smiling. Not a tight smile of frustration as she'd expected, but a relaxed, self-confident grin.

"What?"

"We agree. What we just . . . experienced . . . was fantastic. Just think," Drew said smoothly, "a few weeks earlier, or later, and we might have missed all those magnificent blooms."

"Oh . . . yes . . . I agree," was her faltering response. But, to what, she still wasn't quite sure.

"Thought so." Drew smiled.

Laine all but hopped out of her seat as the tour bus drew to a halt in the Tulum marketplace. A blast of air, hotter and more humid than that in the bus, hit her full force as she stepped from the antiquated vehicle. A groan of protest escaped from her lips. That's all she needed — something else to elevate her temperature! The original source of her heated concern appeared at her elbow.

"How about a little something to cool us down?" Drew asked solicitously. Her head snapped around and Laine encountered the same roguish twinkle she'd seen earlier. Suddenly his thick-fringed lashes lowered to obscure one blue eye in a blatant wink. "Be right back."

The moment Drew turned away from Laine he began scanning the crowd of tourists for the stranger. He'd caught a glimpse of the man, dressed in jeans, faded cotton shirt and Panama hat, as they got off the bus, but not since. Throngs of people milled around the market stalls, making it difficult to spot individuals. After a few moments with no success, Drew decided the man had either left the area or was taking great pains not to be seen. Either way, he didn't like having to table the search until later. The sooner he found out why the man was following him, the better he would feel. By the time Drew returned with icy colas, Laine had recovered from the incident on the bus and was scribbling furiously in a small notebook. Silently she accepted the cold drink, ignoring Drew's irritating self-satisfied grin.

"What's in the notebook?" he inquired between gulps of the soft drink.

"Notes." Intentionally, Laine's response was as frosty as the bottle in her hand. The need to keep him at arm's reach had become paramount. It helped to remind herself that the tour was supposed to be business, but Drew's proximity threatened her resolve. She headed toward the cluster of small open-front shops, determined to maintain a safe distance.

The heat grew more unbearable. After only a few minutes without the protection of the marketplace's thatched roof, a river of perspiration coursed down Laine's slender neck to trickle between her breasts. The swimsuit beneath her shorts and cotton top clung to her moist body. As she and Drew joined the other tourists making their way up a short set of stairs to the ruins, Laine felt suffocated. And Drew's repeated assistance helping her over a boulder, down a dirt path, across crumbling steps as they meandered through the ancient stone structures didn't help at all.

While they strolled and listened to the guide's rambling discourse on the history of Tulum, Laine's pen flew over the pages of her notebook, recording information for convention mail-outs. Always a history buff, she was enthralled as the guide warmed to his subject. Built on a rampart, Tulum, one of the largest of four thousand Mayan ruins, had once been a seaside resort and boasted some of the best-preserved, preclassical stone buildings in Mexico. Many bore faces chiseled in profile on each of the four corners. The intricate stone carvings in themselves were fascinating pieces of art. The fact that such pieces were common not only to public buildings but to private dwellings as well was astounding.

Raphael's thickly accented commentary was punctuated by buzzing voices and flashing cameras. A characteristically American "Rats!" or words to that effect, proved to be the only complaint when the guide informed the group that flashbulbs were prohibited inside the stone buildings, particularly where a magnificent etching was visible behind iron bars. The flashes, Raphael explained, tended to bleach out and destroy the color in the stone. Laine diligently attempted to record as much as she could, keeping a steady pace until a strong, tanned finger tapped her on the shoulder.

"Impressed?" Drew's voice, deep and mellow, drifted over her like a cool breeze.

Laine looked into his fabulous blue eyes and sighed. *Definitely, but not only with an archaeological site.* No female in her right mind could ever describe the "site" of Drew Kenyon as unimpressive. Unwilling to voice her thoughts, she shrugged, then frowned.

The same tanned finger crooked and his husky voice softly commanded, "Follow me." Drew headed for the largest Mayan temple, which rose like a fat gray arrow pointing to the sun.

Drew's purposeful strides carried him past the temple where he veered to the left. Without warning, he halted. Hands on his hips, he turned to watch her close the distance between them. Head down to watch her footing, outstretched arms waving to maintain balance over the rocky terrain, Laine ran full tilt into Drew's stationary frame.

In a flash, his arm snaked around her waist and brought her full against him, nearly lifting her off the ground. Laine gave a startled yelp as the collision, then rescue, positioned her steadfastly between his firmly planted feet, their bodies breast to chest, pelvis to pelvis.

"Sorry, I got ahead of you," Drew's cola-scented breath danced across her upturned face. Laine's eyelashes fluttered in response. Fingers splayed, she felt his big hands move up her narrow back and on to her shoulders.

Every inch of skin covering Laine's frame was tingling — contaminated with radioactive isotopes of desire for the man who held her. Instinctively, she anchored herself by sliding her hands from his biceps to his neck.

"Guess you weren't as far behind as I thought." His voice

seemed to match her body, quiver for quiver, as he reluctantly stepped back. "I want to show you something," he said huskily, then took another step away from Laine just for good measure.

Laine stood rooted to the spot where Drew had placed her, struggling to reduce her galloping pulse rate to a sedate trot. Only moderately successful, she finally nodded her agreement. Whatever view he wanted her to see would have to be spectacular to surpass the one she beheld each time she looked at him. Placing her hand gingerly in his, he led her down a narrow path overshadowed by thick foliage. The wide green leaves of the tropical plants grazed Laine's bare legs and brushed the crown of her head. She wondered where in the world they were going — not that she really cared as long as they went together. Grudgingly she admitted that she was already so involved with Drew she couldn't think straight. How much longer before she went completely bonkers and fell head over heels in love with the man?

Suddenly, Drew executed a short, firm tug, pulling Laine out of the jungle and her reverie and into a small piece of heaven.

The breeze off the water blew across her face and torso, lifting her spirits, just as Drew was lifting her body to a dizzying perch on a rocky ledge. Laine's sharp, indrawn breath accompanied her expression of wide-eyed wonder at the panorama of nature displayed before them.

The sun bedazzled a small cove one hundred feet below, flaunting a semicircle of sand so white the sight was painful to view except through shielding lashes. The beach was enfolded in the cliff's strong rock arms, while being continually soothed by the tide's tranquil, aquamarine caresses.

Laine and Drew absorbed the beauty and grandeur of the awe-inspiring scene. Instinctively, Drew stepped behind Laine and wrapped his arms around her, his chin resting in the crown of soft curls atop her head. Just as instinctively, Laine nestled into his embrace. They didn't kiss, or caress — simply held each other, moved beyond mere words by the beauty of nature and the shared experience.

Laine felt secure — safe and contented to be earthbound in Drew's arms. At the same time she felt free, unfettered — as if soaring gloriously like a seagull on updrafts. For Laine, the depth of emotion welling within her was awesome, exhilarating, yet frightening because it centered on the man holding her. She couldn't renounce the sensation that she was inexorably bound to this man. But where would it lead, this union of souls? Was it possible she had found the one man with whom she could share her deepest self?

Because the questions themselves were devastating enough, Laine refused even to consider the answers. Instead, she shut off her conscious thoughts and, in doing so, unwittingly threw open the door to her heart.

A heady exhilaration raced through Drew's bloodstream. His spirit soared, his heart swelled with a secret splendor he feared to name. He closed his eyes and sighed, knowing that if life on earth ended at that precise moment he would die a happy man. He'd been given a glimpse of paradise, but only because he held an angel.

Laine rotated in the circle of Drew's embrace, buried her nose into his shirt front, wreathed his waist with her arms and gave him a fierce hug. She wanted to convey her feelings, but mere words seemed pitifully inadequate. Then his gentle fingers began to stroke her cheek, his knuckles grazing her face in an endearing expression of understanding.

All the tender words in the world could not have been as eloquent as his one loving touch.

Thus they stood for minutes — hours — days? Neither seemed to know or care. But inevitably, the outside world intruded, as fellow tourists ambled closer and closer to their private pinnacle. By tacit consent, they ended the embrace and made their way silently back to reality.

As they stepped back on the pathway Drew caught sight of the man in the Panama hat standing by the crumbling temple at the bottom of the path.

"I could use another cold drink. How about you?" Holding her hand he suddenly changed direction and led her toward a bench beneath a towering palm tree.

"No, thanks, I —"

"Wait right here in the shade. I'll be back in a minute."

Laine watched him disappear, wondering if he too had been a little frightened by the intimacy of the past few moments. Lord knew, the emotions sweeping through her had scared her silly. Perhaps this was his way of giving them both some time to regain a sense of balance. A small but welcome breeze stirred and she leaned back against the tree to wait.

Drew hated leaving Laine so abruptly, but he had to find out what the mystery man wanted and who had sent him. Walking as rapidly as he could without arousing suspicion, he wove his way through the groups of sun-weary tourists. But his prey was too quick. Just as Drew maneuvered his way clear of the crowd, the man vanished around the side of the ruins and into the jungle.

Dammit! Drew stopped at the edge of the dense foliage for only a split second before plunging in after the man. Almost as soon as the clinging vegetation converged around him, memories of another time, another jungle, closed in too. The smell, dank and cloying with the fragrance of jungle blooms, and even the feel of the earth, soft and spongy beneath his feet, were reminiscent of that other time. Now, as then, he was the hunter, alert for the sounds and movements of his quarry. From the direction they were headed, Drew surmised they would eventually end up on the beach below the cliffs. He'd seen the beach dotted with sun worshipers and knew that once out of the jungle, he would have difficulty with a confrontation.

Yanking and slapping vines and brush out of his way he struggled, the sound of surf coming closer and closer. Just as the foliage began to thin out, Drew saw the Panama. With a knowledge born of practice he crouched and moved swiftly, circling to the left. At the point where lush green ended and white sand began, Drew sprang, catching his prey from behind. In a flash Drew's forearm was a steel bar across the man's throat. A sudden jerk sent the Panama flying.

"Who the hell are you and why are you following me?"

"No. No . . . *habla* English, *señor,*" came the choked response. Two darkly tanned hands clawed at Drew's rigid forearm.

"The hell you don't! Who's paying you? Tell me, dammit, or I'll break your neck." Drew's voice was deadly calm.

"*¡Por . . . favor!*" The choked voice was barely a whisper. "Do . . . not . . . hurt me, *señor*. Ple-e-ease."

"You don't know what hurt is unless you tell me what I need to know." The increased pressure of Drew's arm against the man's Adam's apple brought on another spasm of choking. "Tell me."

"*Sí, sí.* A man. Paid . . . me."

"Who paid you?"

"Don't . . . know —"

Suddenly, a beach ball came whizzing through the air and landed less than four feet from where the antagonists stood. Playful squeals increased in volume as several youngsters scrambled for the toy.

Drew quickly slackened his hold. If the children looked closely the squeals might become screams. Careful to keep his arm on his captive's shoulder, he attempted to turn both of them away. As he did, the other man broke free and ran straight for the group of children.

"Here *niños*," he croaked as he scooped up the beach ball and presented it to a blond, freckle-faced preschooler. The next second he dashed across the beach without a backward glance at his attacker.

Drew's doubled-up fist smacked the center of his palm. *Damn! Someone's having me tailed! But who! And why?* A man didn't serve two tours of duty in Vietnam and eight years working for the CIA without making some enemies. His list was probably as long as his arm even though he'd been out of the intelligence business for over two years. Who could be interested in him now? Drew's next thought sent him dashing out of the jungle and up the beach, but not in pursuit. As he raced up the path leading back to the ruins only one thought was uppermost in his mind.

If someone was watching him, they were also watching Laine.

He was breathing hard by the time he reached her.

"Where's your drink?" A touch of annoyance colored her voice.

"My what?"

"I thought you went to get a soda." Quizzically, she eyed his obvious signs of physical exertion.

"I finished it." His breathing began to normalize.

"You were gone so long I thought you had forgotten about me."

Drew looked at her and an almost nauseous wave of relief surged over him. *Thank God she's all right. If anything had happened to her —*

"Drew? Are you okay?" She rose from the bench and touched his cheek.

Ignoring her question, he turned his head and kissed the soft center of her palm. "Forgetting about you is impossible.

Thanks for waiting for me."

"Of course, but —"

Abruptly, he slipped an arm about her waist, pulled her to him and kissed her hard. He seemed almost as surprised as she was when he lifted his mouth from hers a second or two later.

"I think . . . we'd better get back to the bus," he said, frowning.

The return bus ride bore no resemblance to the outbound trip. Laine was, if possible, more confused than ever. Drew was remote.

I never should have kissed her. Not like that, hard and rough. But he hadn't been able to help himself. It had been all he could do not to yank her up off that bench and squeeze her until she was as breathless as he was. He'd known fear more times than he cared to count, but never, never like what he'd experienced at the thought of someone harming her. Just remembering how scared he'd been made him sick to his stomach. Tomorrow he would call Rankin and see if he could get some answers. Until then, he was torn between desperately needing to be with Laine and feeling she might be safer without his company. For perhaps the first time, Drew understood why Rankin preferred to work with unmarried, unattached agents. Caring about someone made you vulnerable; and for an agent, vulnerability was deadly.

By the time they disembarked at the hotel, the sun had relented its blistering grasp on Cancún and was preparing to sizzle into the Caribbean, extinguishing itself for another day. Both Laine and Drew were subdued.

Since the incident on the cliff, his attitude toward her had changed. He acted cool, almost indifferent. If he hadn't kissed her the way he had — No, she assured herself, the kiss had been anything but indifferent. Laine finally decided that he was

91

having as much trouble as she was in trying to define emotions and desires. Perhaps he was having second thoughts.

The polite silence was unendurable by the time he left her at her door. Laine wondered if their hoped-for relationship was ending before it had really begun.

Chapter 6

A few hours later, the persistent ringing of her phone commanded Laine's scrambling exit from the shower.

"Hello."

"Have dinner with me tonight?" the familiar voice at the other end coaxed. "Please, say yes."

No one said please the way he did. Just the right touch of sincerity mixed with longing flowed through his voice.

Laine's heart sang "Yes, a thousand times yes," and her mind shouted "No, you're asking for trouble." Being with Drew was an emotional roller-coaster ride — breathless excitement one minute, scared witless by the same excitement the next. Laine's mind reasoned that for the sake of her own sanity she should decline.

"Drew, I'm . . . not sure —"

"I am. Sure enough for both of us."

A fresh towel hugging the front of her damp body absorbed the moisture there, but left water trickling down her back to pool briefly in the hollow above her buttock before sliding the length of slim legs. Her senses replaced the beads of water with strong, firm, masculine hands and fingers.

She sighed, the soft sound drifting over the telephone line. Drew shuddered, pressing the phone to his ear as though her breath had actually touched him.

"Everything is moving so fast and —"

"And I promised to let you set the pace, didn't I. Does this mean 'no' to dinner?"

"It means 'yes' . . . to dinner."

"A nice, s-l-o-w dinner, right?"

"You think we can do that?" He didn't miss the we.

"I think we can do anything we set our minds to." And hearts, he wanted to add. "If it's slow and easy you want, slow and easy you get." The husky vibrations in his voice gave the words a double meaning. "Do you like to dance?"

"Yes." She very much liked the idea of spending time in his arms.

"Good, then I'll find someplace quiet with good food and lots of sweet music. We can dance the night away."

Forty-five minutes later, studying her reflection in a full-length mirror, Laine applauded her wardrobe decisions for what she felt would be a special evening. The sparkling-white nautically accoutred sundress was a discreet halter style. Newly purchased, its soft cotton bodice embraced her narrow midriff, then cupped her breasts enticingly. The neckline extended into a sailor collar that partially covered her back, which was otherwise bare to the waist. The collar, hem and belt were piped in navy. White sandals, gold anchor-shaped earrings and a single gold chain at her neck completed the outfit. Cool, dressy, and not too much skin showing. She pivoted for a back view and her eyes widened at the way the fabric dipped seductively to the waist. *Well, two out of three isn't bad.*

The restaurant was small, quiet, and intimate — exactly how Laine felt standing next to Drew while they waited for the maître d' to appear. Head at a slight tilt, she surveyed the profile of her handsome escort. Did he really get better-looking every time she saw him, or was her imagination working overtime?

Tonight, a pale-blue oxford-cloth shirt encased the shoulders she so admired and khaki-colored slacks hugged the hips she remembered pressing against her so enticingly. She was green with envy — the blue and khaki touched him everywhere she longed to.

Her thoughts were interrupted by the arrival of the headwaiter. Laine emitted a tiny gasp of delighted surprise when they were ushered into an open-air patio. Several small tables, each partially surrounded by lush palms, ferns and overhanging banyan trees, nestled in the tropical garden. Candles flickered atop snow-white tablecloths, stars twinkled overhead in a black velvet sky and the soft sounds of piano music drifted through the garden on a gentle breeze.

Like the setting, Laine was enchanted, wrapped in a romantic aura surrounding just the two of them. And Drew . . .

Drew was perfect. Charming, attentive, he adroitly kept the conversation light and interesting, but benign. Over a delicious meal of seafood curry served in coconut shells, they talked about the ambience of the restaurant, the weather. They spoke of everything except the one thing foremost in their minds — each other. The experience in Tulum had marked a turning point in their relationship and neither seemed quite sure of the next step.

Drew innocuously swirled brandy in a snifter as the conversation ebbed to a standstill. Now, with only the tinkling of glasses and murmuring voices of other diners in the background, the silence seemed to magnify. He sipped the liqueur, then watched the amber liquid slowly paint the sides of the glass. For the first time in his memory he was uncomfortable with a woman. But Laine wasn't just any woman, she was his woman. That's how he'd come to think of her now — his. Not so much with an attitude of possessiveness, but of rightness. Their being together was right. No matter what arguments he gave himself, it always came back to one inescapable fact: he wanted her. In his bed, in his life, in his heart.

"Shall we dance?" Drew's soft question floated across to Laine; her heart skipped several beats before she nodded her acceptance. Wordlessly, they rose in unison and Drew reached out to take her hand.

The dance floor, partially hidden at the opposite end of the garden, was small and uncrowded. As they drew near, the mellow notes of the piano player's rendition of "The Entertainer" faded to completion. Drew pulled Laine into his arms as the music resumed, accompanied by the vocalist's soothing baritone voice. The words sang of a man doubting he would ever find anyone. Then, miraculously, life favored him and he knew he'd found the one he could love always.

Laine sighed and nestled into Drew's embrace as they glided across the floor, lost in the music, in the words, in each other. Her body pressed to his, they moved together in seductive synchronization, the slow beat of the poignant tune carrying them further and further into a world known only to lovers. She wished the music were endless. She wanted never to leave the haven of his arms.

Drew cradled Laine close as their bodies swayed to the music. One hand caressed the small of her back, the other tucked her right hand to his chest, near his heart. His thumb gently stroked the center of her palm. The loneliness, so long a part of him, was gone. For the time being he wanted to forget about mystery men and juries and the rest of the world. He was right where he wanted to be and he prayed the dance might last forever so he would never have to let her go.

How had he been granted this supreme stroke of luck? What ancient god of love had smiled on him and sent the one woman with the power to make his life complete? He suddenly realized how much she had altered his existence in so short a time. His life before Laine seemed dull and colorless in comparison. Who was he kidding? In the past few days she had become his life.

Slipping his hand from hers he wrapped his arms around her slender body in a gently possessive embrace. He couldn't touch her enough, hold her enough.

Laine's arms wreathed his neck, her cheek rested over his

heart, which beat in time with hers. They danced as lovers had since the dawn of time — entwined, attuned, enraptured, oblivious to the outside world.

The song ended, but the same mythical god who sent lovers to one another must still have been on guard because the singer moved smoothly into another ballad, then still another. Tender music for a night made for tenderness. The singer's final sweet note faded into silence and they stood without moving for long seconds, then slowly, reluctantly, parted.

"Thank you," Laine murmured. "That was . . . perfect."

Her words were sunlight warming his heart. "You were perfect. Light as a feather in my arms and smooth as silk."

"I'm afraid you give me too much credit," she returned modestly.

"I could never give you too much of anything."

She couldn't think straight when he talked like that. As much as she thrilled to the excitement he promised with every touch, she feared such promises would be short-lived. Once before, she'd succumbed to the magical excitement only to be left with her heart in pieces. Drew, the night, the music — everything was too wonderful; too much, too fast.

Drew sensed her hesitation even before she slipped her hand from his. He knew she was struggling with her emotions, knew she was unaccustomed to his brand of pursuit. And he also realized that the advance and retreat he had made earlier that day confused her.

A long history of instantaneous and often life-altering decisions gave Drew the advantage of knowing his course. Determination and confidence had always served him well in obtaining his goal. This time, the objective was not a fleeting moment of satisfaction, but a lifetime of happiness. Drew knew he was sending her mixed messages but until he could find out who was having him followed, she was as much at risk as he.

As they neared their table, he announced wistfully, "It's late, we should be starting back."

"Yes." She felt bereft without his arms about her, but agreed. "I guess today took a lot more out of me than I realized." She was tired, but her fatigue had nothing to do with lingering effects of the sun. Laine was beginning to realize that her exhaustion was a direct result of resisting her feelings for Drew. She wasn't fighting him; she was fighting herself — and losing.

Star-studded and sultry, the night lost some of its magic as the taxi whizzed along *Paseo Kukul-Can* toward the hotel and the end of their evening. Positioned as they were on opposite sides of the back seat, they could have been strangers rather than potential lovers. Each stared out their respective windows, unmindful of the soft tropical night.

For years Drew had promised himself no entanglements, never to subject any woman to his erratic lifestyle. Yet, he'd started to break those promises almost from the minute he had set eyes on Laine. He was becoming obsessed with her and his obsession made him impetuous — a dangerous state of mind.

Out of the corner of his eye, he noted the rise and fall of her breasts as she sighed deeply. Her forearm was flat against the door's armrest and her fingertips trailed restlessly across the frayed padding. Moonlight lent her face a pearlescent glow, and she looked like a delicate porcelain figurine wrought by the hands of an incredibly sensitive artist. His breath caught in his throat. Her beauty was almost ethereal. A longing for all that she was shot into his heart.

He loved her.

How long ago it had begun, he didn't know. It was enough that he loved her — immeasurably, unconditionally and indefinitely. A treasure worth seeking; and he loved her too much to risk losing her.

Laine stole a quick look at Drew, then averted her gaze before he could catch her. He seemed more than content with the distance between them, figuratively as well as literally. She'd asked him to slow down and he was definitely acceding to her wishes. So why was she so miserable? Because, for a brief span of time tonight she'd been in heaven, floating like an angel on a cloud of happiness within the circle of his arms, and now she felt that happiness slipping away — and the fault was her own. Being deprived of Drew's loving attention was more painful than Laine could ever have imagined. Without his touch, his warm smile and soothing voice, she felt cheated, lost.

She alone was responsible for her inability to take the exceptional chance life was offering her. Why did she hold herself away from this man who had become so precious to her, she couldn't bear to think of losing him? Hurtful memories of her marriage sprang to mind. Greg had told her almost daily how much he loved her and, like a naive kid, Laine believed that saying the words made them true. Drew had never mentioned love; but then Drew was nothing like her ex-husband, and never would be. What existed between them was different, theirs alone. Was it worth a few risks, a small tempest in Eden, even some heartache? She wouldn't know until she tried. Turning toward him, she discovered that he was watching her.

"Would you mind if I asked the driver to pull over?" she asked nervously. "It's only a few blocks back to the hotel. We could walk the rest of the way."

"If you like."

As they watched the red taillights of the taxi disappear from view, Laine entwined her fingers with Drew's. She was hanging

99

on to hope by a slender thread and knew she was about to take a gigantic gamble.

"Have you —" she faltered.

"Changed my mind? Decided I don't want you?"

She stared up into his handsome face, tempted to ask where he kept his crystal ball, then decided he probably didn't need one. Hadn't Greg always said she wore her heart on her sleeve? Could Drew see how vulnerable she was right now? He'd been honest with her from the very beginning. Did she have the courage to match his honesty?

"We made no promises."

"Only to give ourselves time to get to know one another."

"Until a week ago we were strangers," she reminded him.

"Were we strangers? Think about it, Laine. Didn't we each recognize in the other something we'd been searching for?"

Unable to deny the truth of his statement, she looked down at the asphalt beneath their feet. "I know very little about you," she hedged.

"What do you want to know?"

Laine had no way of understanding what the offer to talk about himself had cost Drew. She only heard another example of the integrity he seemed to possess in unlimited quantities.

"Did it ever occur to you that maybe there's something you should know about me?" She was determined to match his directness.

"I know all I need to know."

"Did you know I'd been married before?" Her voice was shaky.

"Yes."

Laine's head snapped around and she stared at him. The shock had backfired. "You . . . but I never told —"

"I read the questionnaire you filled out when you were

100

selected for grand jury service."

"Oh."

"Did you think your having been married would make a difference?"

"No. I . . ." She tried to look away, but he captured her chin between his thumb and index finger.

"Then tell me what's bothering you."

Her thick eyelashes fluttered slightly and her slender frame almost wilted with released tension.

"I'm afraid."

"Of me?"

"No, of me. I don't know myself when I'm with you." It was true. With intimate caresses and whispered words, he'd revealed dimensions of herself she'd never known existed.

"You're my lovely Laine." Tenderly he smoothed back a curl tossed across her cheek by the night breezes.

"I want to be."

"But you're not sure?"

She shook her head from side to side slowly, moisture building in the corners her eyes. At last, he pulled her into his embrace and held her against him.

"Your divorce was painful, wasn't it?"

She nodded, her cheek next to his rapidly beating heart.

"Was marriage so bad?"

"Not at first." Her warm breath fanned his shirt. "In the beginning it was wonderful and always, always fun. I was so eager to please him I didn't realize having fun was his only ambition. Greg was childish and self-centered; and I was supposed to be mother and lover. But after a while I wasn't enough. I came home early from a business trip to discover he'd found another playmate."

His arms tightened around her waist. "I could kill him for hurting you."

"I almost forgave him. I should say, he almost talked me into forgiving. Then, quite by accident, I discovered Greg's real love in life. Flashy women and cars were only fuel to keep him revved up for the real high. Gambling. He couldn't resist betting, on anything. I knew he lived in the fast lane, or on the edge anyway. When we first met, I thought his way of life sounded exciting, attractive. But there is nothing attractive about wondering if the next check you write the grocery store will bounce.

"The worst part," she said with a sniff, "was that I blamed myself for most of our problems — I wasn't understanding enough; my career demanded too much of my time. Greg needed something I couldn't give him. I wanted so badly for my marriage to work, Drew, that I gave up part of myself trying. After the divorce my self-image was so damaged I barely recognized myself."

"Now you don't trust your emotions anymore."

She nodded her head, offering him a tentative smile. "Sometimes when we're together, I have the feeling I'm walking a tightrope."

"I know."

She'd spoken her fears out loud and he was still holding her as if he never intended to let her go. She drew a full draught of courage from his reassuring touch.

"I want you, Drew."

"Oh, God. I want you too. So much."

Drew realized how difficult it was for Laine to open up her soul, to allow him to see inside. The pain of having to turn his back on her trusting gesture would be killing, but he had to, for her sake. For all he knew, they were being watched right now. And the kind of people who paid to know his whereabouts were not interested in sending him a birthday card. Some of them played for keeps. He couldn't risk Laine being hurt because someone was trying to get to him.

They stood for several moments, holding each other. Then he tucked her securely to his side and they began to walk leisurely along the narrow path around the lagoon, toward their hotel.

Alone in her room, an hour after Drew's sweetly murmured "Good night," Laine was still in a state of semishock. After declaring her desire, she had half expected — no, fully expected — the evening to end differently. It hadn't and she felt hurt . . . and angry. He had stated point-blank that he wanted to make love to her, yet he had walked away from her as though it were the last thing on his mind. First he does, then he doesn't. Laine punched her pillow in frustration.

Now she courted slumber like a relentless suitor, but to no avail. Finally, abandoning the effort altogether, she threw back the rumpled sheets, discarded her nightgown and stomped to the closet. A walk along the beach would clear her head, she decided. She sought and found a Mexican-crafted caftan in gauzy, peach-colored muslin. Ignoring her bra, Laine slipped quickly into bikini panties, then into the flowing folds of the caftan.

Seconds later, the door clicked shut behind her as she made her way toward the elevator. She reached to press the indicator and her hand froze. A fraction of an inch from the tip of her finger, the unlit arrow pointed upward. Up or down? Yes or no? On an impulse, an unsteady index finger touched the "up" arrow.

Two flights up, on the fourth floor, a not-so-steady masculine hand all but pounded the "down" button.

Chapter 7

"Damn!" Drew's curse bounced off the walls of the empty elevator. Unconsciously, he had selected Laine's floor. Or was his choice a Freudian slip of the finger? The muscles in his neck were taut with tension. He glanced up and saw the lighted numerals flash the elevator's descent: three, two. The other elevator whirrred past on its ascent. His cubicle stopped with a jerk and the door yawned open to the second floor.

Lord, but he was tempted! Her room was only a few yards down the carpeted corridor. So close. Too close. A warning bell shrilled in Drew's ear, signaling that the doors had remained open too long. With a blistering oath he jabbed the first-floor circle. *I could use a good stiff drink.* As he exited the elevator, he longingly eyed the still-active poolside bar. Couples danced intimately, glasses tinkled and a woman's musical laughter floated to him on the breeze.

Above, on the fourth floor, the elevator doors swooshed open and Laine stared into the empty hallway. She hesitated for a moment, then pressed "one." No. He'd made his position very clear by walking away tonight. She couldn't go to him now. The elevator obeyed her command and swooped downward.

The festive customers of the softly lit poolside bar drew only minuscule notice from Laine as she crossed the patio and descended several stone steps to the beach. Her footprints in the still-warm sand marked her path toward the beckoning sound of the surf. Strolling along the water's edge, she gazed out across the rolling waves and let the eloquent silence of the night envelop her. The soft murmur of the ocean failed to soothe her. Nothing could assuage the sting of Drew's rejection.

In the light wind the soft folds of her caftan swirled and

lapped at her slender frame in almost-perfect unison with the waves against the sand. The repeated ebb and flow of the garment had an unusually erotic effect on Laine. Her skin tingled as the caftan caressed her body like a lover's touch. Drew's touch. Laine's ill temper, aggravated by sexual tension, produced a low-boiling frustration.

She had no idea how far she had traveled on her midnight outing when she glanced up and stopped dead in her tracks. Barely thirty feet away, a boulder jutted out into the water resembling the mammoth hull of a broken and abandoned ship.

On the highest point of the "bow," looking out to sea, sat Drew. Bare-legged and bare-chested, his profile was a study in form and light. One leg hung over the rim of the rocky ledge just far enough so that continual bursts of foamy spray teased the frayed hem of his denim cutoffs. Illumination from a full moon combined with a subliminal glow from the hotel lighting infused the spume with iridescence. Saltwater beads sparkled with a metallic glitter on Drew's body. One arm, crooked at the elbow, held his other leg, which was bent at the knee to form a prop for his chin. The wind choreographed his hair, sending tendrils dancing across his forehead as he stared out to sea.

Laine's heart almost burst with joy until she remembered how she'd been agonizing over his well-delivered cold shoulder. Quickly she turned and headed back up the beach.

A movement out of the corner of his eye caught Drew's attention and a deep frown insinuated its way across his forehead. His solitude disturbed, he rose and propelled himself from his perch to the sand. He crammed his hands into the pockets of his shorts, took a step forward, glanced up, then came to an abrupt halt. With a suddenly erratic beat, his heart started to batter his chest wall.

"Laine?"

She ignored his call and quickened her step.

"Laine!" A heartbeat later she was whirled around to face him. "Why did you run away?"

In her state of agitation, the puzzled expression on his face and the dispassionate tone in his voice fanned her smoldering emotions.

"I could ask you the same question," she snapped.

He didn't even pretend to misunderstand. "Laine, I'm sorry. I know how my behavior must look —"

"It looks like you've changed your mind, that's all." Her voice sharpened and her temper, once vented, raged unreasonably. "Men like you change your mind as easily as you change your shirt. I should have known better."

"What do you mean, 'men like me'?" He was prepared to explain and sympathize, but he wasn't prepared for her wrath. Perhaps in defense, her unreasonable outburst triggered a similar response in him. Unleashed, his frustrations rolled forth in anger. "Just exactly what kind of a man do you think I am?"

"You're . . . you're sophisticated, a smooth talker —"

"And therefore not to be trusted?"

"Yes!" She tried to break away, but he held her fast.

"And you don't want explanations."

"No!"

"You don't know what you want!"

"Me!" she screeched. "If that's not the pot calling the kettle black! You run hot and cold, Drew Kenyon. One minute you're practically seducing me and the next, you act as if you couldn't care less!" She jerked herself free and started to run. He caught her before she took two steps.

"You want me to make up my mind. All right, consider it done. Obviously you don't care for cold. Let's see how you like hot."

Without warning his mouth took hers in a brutal kiss. She

106

gasped for air and he took full advantage. His tongue was a savage intruder, tameless, insisting she yield to him. Instinctively, she shrugged. Forceful arms encompassed her shoulders and one hip, crushing her to him. She whimpered a protest.

Abruptly, the pressure against her mouth changed. Where before he had been vicious, he was now tender. Where before he had demanded, he now begged, his tongue soothing the kiss-bruised softness he had violated. Her resistance dissolved like cotton candy in a hard rain. She kissed him back, well and passionately.

"Laine, Laine," he whispered, at last pulling his mouth from hers. "My God, I never meant to hurt you. Please forgive me."

"It's all right. No one is to blame and I know you would never hurt me."

"I only wanted to keep you safe. I didn't think you'd need protection from me."

"Drew, don't."

"I can't believe my cruelty —"

"Please, don't." She kissed his cheek.

"Laine." His deep voice faltered slightly as he placed hot, fleeting kisses at the corner of her mouth, her chin, her jaw. "You're so sweet, so soft. How could you even think I don't want you? I've gone mad wanting to make love to you."

For a long moment he stared into her face, his heated gaze flashing like summer lightning. Then his hands slid up her shoulders, caressed her neck and threaded through her hair. As he had longed to do the first time he saw her, he crushed the mass of silken curls in his hands. At his gentle tug, her head fell back, offering up her parted lips.

"I need you," he said as his mouth came down on hers in another soul-searing kiss. "Oh, God, how I need you."

Laine was on fire, consumed from the soles of her feet to the top of her head in a wild, sweet inferno. With a soft moan, she wrapped slender arms around his neck and pressed her abdomen against the ridge beneath his jeans. Her tongue met his, stroke for stroke. Her body ached for his touch.

"And I need you," she whispered urgently.

"Are you sure?"

"Yes."

"I don't want you to have any regrets."

She buried her face in the hollow of his throat and sighed. "No regrets."

Of one mind, they walked across the sand. Laine barely remembered leaving the beach, or taking the elevator, or stepping inside Drew's room. All she knew, or cared about, was that the instant the door closed she was in his arms again.

He released her only long enough to whip the caftan from her slender body, revealing her naked save for the scant triangle of silk. Every nerve in her body quivered with delicious anticipation as he took a step back, slowly wadded the fabric into a ball, then pitched it across the room.

As long as he lived, Drew knew he would remember her as she was now: a slender goddess, all soft and golden. He would never have enough of looking at her, being with her. She was breathtaking. Creamy breasts; flat, smooth stomach; auburn nest of curls nearly invisible beneath the enticing bit of silk; long, shapely legs. He reached out and covered a perfect breast with his hand. A ragged half-sigh, half-moan issued from her lips and she swayed into him.

As they moved toward the bed, her desperate fingers worked with limited results at the snap of his cutoffs, becoming frantic to eliminate the barriers between them, urgent to feel all of him against all of her. A second later, the remaining articles of clothing joined the caftan.

Amid the soft sheets they were simply man and woman, flesh to flesh.

"Sweet," Drew murmured nipping at the tender skin of her neck. "Unbelievably, incredibly sweet. I want to taste all of you. Feel your sweetness surround me. Warm. Wonderful." His voice vibrated against her throat. Erratic, jangling electric impulses shot through every nerve in her body. Mental strings, once having restrained her desire, came untied to wave in the breeze like so much crepe paper after a parade, their importance lost in the tumult of excitement.

She made a soft mewing sound and reached to pull him closer. He captured her hand in midair. Lacing his fingers through hers, he laid their clasped hands on the pillow just above her dark curls and shook his head solemnly. "We have all night."

Starting at the hollow of her throat, he began to kiss her. Across her collarbone, over her shoulder, around the nape of her neck. As a jeweler creates a necklace of priceless pearls, stringing each one with love and care, he encircled her neck with soft kisses.

She sighed.

Moving his head only inches lower, he kissed a crescent from one shoulder, across the swell of her breasts, to the other shoulder.

She moaned.

Again, kisses spanned her ribcage, brushing the underside of her breasts with his warm lips.

She whimpered.

From one satiny hip, to the other, dipping to circle her navel with his moist tongue, he kissed her.

"I want you. Please, Drew, don't make me wait. Love me now," she begged. With a surrendering groan he raised himself up and slipped into her honeyed warmth.

Then they were complete. Two halves fitted together to make a whole.

Drew held himself still for a moment, content to be sheathed in her liquid fire. Then he began to love her, worship her slowly . . . at first.

"Ah-h . . . perfect," came his hoarsely whispered praise as his tongue danced along her throat and up to her waiting mouth. "Laine . . . you . . . take me . . . to paradise."

She arched her body and Drew slid his big hands beneath her hips, holding her suspended in space and time while he stroked deeply, the tempo increasing with each movement. She met him thrust for thrust, not content merely to receive but also wanting to give . . . everything.

They moved in unison, sharing the wondrous ascent, awed by the power and depth of what they were experiencing. When at last they reached the summit and teetered on the brink of release for one split second in time, the world was a brilliant, glowing star. Then the star "novaed," bursting from within, showering them with joy beyond their wildest imaginings and with love beyond their sweetest dreams.

Minutes, days, years later, they drifted back to reality, floating slowly through the same space that moments before had been a tumultuous storm. They settled gently to earth into the hazy void following a raging tornado of feelings and emotions.

"I've never . . ."

"Neither have I." He confirmed her unfinished proclamation. "Not like this, never like this. Beautiful."

Beneath her ear the sound of his heartbeat pulsed through her as if it were her own life force and his arms tightened around her. Dual sighs of mutual contentment mingled as sleep wrapped the lovers in shared dreams.

Faint wisps of moonlight diffused throughout the room as the lone figure in the wide bed stirred. Slender arms reached, questing hands searched, as on the fringes of slumber Laine sought the strength and warmth of Drew. She wiggled restlessly in the bed, her body instinctively seeking Drew's. Her hand swept across a vacant expanse of percale and consciousness penetrated her sleep-drugged mind. She sat up among the tousled sheets, searching the dimly lit room. "Drew?"

He stood on the balcony, buttocks resting on the lip of the wrought-iron rail, one foot braced against its flat side. His arms were crossed over his bare chest and a towel was slung enticingly low around his hips. Across the moonlight-dappled room he watched her.

"Drew?"

Three swift strides brought him to her side. With a soft plop, the towel fell to the floor and Drew took his place beside her warm body.

"Where were you?" She wrapped an arm around his waist and snuggled close to him.

He exhaled a long breath and kissed her temple. "On the balcony, watching you. You sleep like a child, all curled on your side, waiting for a good-night kiss." His voice, though gentle, sounded strained and the last traces of drowsiness vanished from Laine's mind.

"Why did you go?" An air of expectancy threaded through the silence that followed.

"To listen to the surf. To think."

"About what?"

"You."

"What about me?"

"About how sweet and beautiful you are. How very warm and giving you are. How very lucky I am to be the one you finally decided to risk sharing yourself with. You've given me a very precious gift, Laine. One I'll always treasure."

Wide-eyed, she searched his expression and found the tender honesty to match his words of silk. That he had known, shared and appreciated what she had given to him as she had to no other was soul-mending.

"Thank you," she murmured, her voice throaty with emotion.

He wanted to tell her how loving her had wiped away so many old hurts, how it had made his past seem unimportant, but it was too soon. Emotions were too fragile. The time would come when he could tell all of it, he knew, but not now. First he had to find out who hired the man in the Panama hat.

"If I said 'My pleasure,' would it sound too macho?" The little-boy smile she loved so much appeared.

"On you, macho looks good."

"Hmm, thanks." He nuzzled her delicate throat.

"My pleasure," she returned softly, squirming and wiggling along his lean frame until she found the exact position where the maximum amount of her flesh touched the maximum amount of his. Her fingers tiptoed across his broad shoulders, up his strong neck. An exploring thumb smoothed a spot just beneath the lobe of his ear. In turn, he caressed a slender hip, kneading the soft flesh beneath his fingers.

"Mmm-m-m, nice." His neck arched to accommodate her touch. "You fascinate me."

"Do I?"

"Yes-s-s," he hissed slowly, as her fingers danced over his shoulders and across his back. "You're the most innocently sensual woman I've ever known. However, if you keep this up, I may have to strike 'innocent.' "

"How can I be innocent and sexy at the same time?" she murmured, more interested in the feel of his skin beneath her fingers.

"Not sexy. Sensual."

"Just to keep the record straight, would you give me your definition of sexy and sensual?" She pulled back and looked

112

at him as though she had some doubts as to his seriousness.

"Sexy is when a woman knows she has what it takes, and showcases it. That kind of blatant appeal may catch my eye, but won't hold my attention." His eyes looked deep into hers. "Sensual is when a woman's sexuality is natural and unassuming, therefore positively deadly to any male over the age of ten." His voice dropped to a husky murmur. "When that kind of woman walks into a room, without even realizing it she makes every male there *know* he's a man. She doesn't use her sensuality. She doesn't have to."

"That's marvelous," she sighed, genuinely impressed with his eloquence.

"And you —" he kissed the hollow of her cheek "are definitely" another kiss "— sensual. When I offer even the tiniest caress, you seem to flower beneath my touch. I feel as if I hold the keys to your soul and can unlock all your mysteries."

"You do." The movement of his lips to her jawline brought a sigh and a smile. "But it's no . . . ah . . ." Laine's voice trailed off briefly as Drew's smooth teeth gently nipped her neck, then journeyed on. "No mystery — simple, logical progression." Her breathing became decidedly shallow.

He raised his head and eyed her quizzically. "I don't think I like my lovemaking referred to as logical," he said, rekindled desire flashing in his azure eyes.

She shook her head slowly. "It's very simple. I crave your touch. Every time you caress me I want more, and more, and . . . See, a logical progression."

Drew shifted his body and brought them nose to nose. "With a very satisfying conclusion." His hands roamed the territory his lips had explored earlier.

"Very."

"Most women even hesitate to admit to such a natural response to a man."

"Most women don't have you for a lover."

"Dear God." His gentle hands cupped her face. "I can't conceive of what my life would be like if I ever lost you."

He looked as though he were weighing the possibility and Laine saw herself reflected in the blue depths — a lonely soul reaching out to another for love and tenderness. Could his life have been as unfulfilled as hers? She wanted to hold him to her breast, not in passion, but in loving comfort.

"Do you know what loneliness, real loneliness, is like?" Drew's eyes clouded, his voice sounded like an echo from an empty tomb.

"Yes. It's feeling you don't belong anywhere . . . to anyone." Laine's soft voice, conveying an infinite compassion, pulled him from his reverie.

He studied her face for several seconds, then kissed her with a savage intensity. She thought she heard him whisper "No more," just before his lips touched hers.

Sunlight poured over the couple beneath the rumpled white sheets like butterscotch syrup over vanilla ice cream. Stirring, Laine and Drew reluctantly surrendered to the encroaching day, snuggling closer, legs entwined.

"Morning."

Laine lifted one eyelid to find Drew smiling at her.

"Hm-m, morning." She flopped over and wiggled her bottom against him, fitting their forms together spoon-fashion.

"If you keep rubbing your delicious little rump against —" she rotated her hips ever so slightly "— we may spend the entire day in this bed."

"The entire day?"

"Every second."

Laine stilled. Drew propped himself on an elbow and looked down at her serene face, lashes resting placidly against her delicate cheek. Still she didn't move. His throat went dry while his forehead dampened with perspiration. Was she having regrets after all?

"Laine?" he asked, barely able to keep the dread in his heart from coloring his voice.

"Sh-h-h. I haven't decided yet."

"D-decided?" Drew's voice was unsteady.

"Whether to spend the whole day in bed." Her eyes remained closed, but she was grinning. "Does the prosecution wish to present evidence to sway the judge's decision?"

Drew collapsed against the pillow with a strangled chuckle that grew into a hearty laugh.

"I'm so delighted I've been able to entertain you," Laine said warily, twisting to face him. "What's so funny?"

"You. Me. I . . . well, for a minute there . . ."

"You were afraid I might be having some qualms." Laine finished softly, realizing that he had a few insecurities of his own. "I meant it when I told you no regrets. How about you? Any second thoughts?"

Her eyes were gentle with understanding. Relief coursed through Drew's body and he gave her one of his dazzling smiles. "Second, third and fourth, and they're all about you and how special I feel when we're together. I'm hooked, lady. All I can do now is throw myself on the mercy of the court and beg for leniency, pleading *causa sine qua non*."

"What does *that* mean?"

"A cause without which the effect in question could not have happened."

"And what does that mean?"

"You turn me on." He pushed back a mass of curls and stroked a silken shoulder.

"Case dismissed," she replied breathlessly.

Many hours passed before feeding the stomach took precedence over nourishing the soul. Finally, hunger forced their return to the real world.

They booked a short cruise to the island of Mujeres and while Laine was dressing, Drew slipped away to the lobby and called Washington. To his disappointment, Rankin was involved in a Senate committee hearing and wouldn't return until the next day. He thought about, then decided against contacting some cronies who might still have information sources. The fewer people involved, the better. So far, he hadn't seen the man in the Panama hat again. In the meantime he would stay alert and keep trying to reach Rankin.

Chapter 8

The glass-bottom trimaran skimmed across the turquoise water, a giant low-flying sea gull. White sails emblazoned with the ship's name *Tiger Prince*, billowed and furled in the trade winds. Laine lay on her stomach near the bow of the ship, the sun baking her svelte body.

"You look like a sleeping, golden goddess." A warm breath tickled her ear. She smiled. "Did I interrupt a lovely dream?"

Laine raised up on her elbows and looked at Drew. If she resembled a goddess, then he most certainly was her counterpart. The male strength, cleanliness and beauty of him was awesome; indeed, he was more handsome than any god.

"I don't need lovely dreams; I have you." A bright flame of desire sprang into her eyes.

Drew gave an anxious little cough and glanced around nervously. "If you keep looking at me that way, we're going to give the other people on this boat an X-rated memory to take home with them." His smoldered with fire and he flashed her a none-too-gentle warning. "Take your pick. Either turn off your motor or take off your clothes."

"Bully," she accused in a low, purposefully seductive voice.

"Have it your way." His lean finger went to the waistband of his swimsuit.

"Drew Kenyon, don't you dare!" Laine twisted and sat bolt upright.

"Chicken." He traced his fingertip across her bottom lip.

"Through and through," she assured him, her body beginning to vibrate with liquid fire. His mouth replaced his finger while his hand seared a path down her arm, onto her hip.

The ship's bell sounded, heralding their arrival on the island.

Drew stared at her parted lips, still moist from his kiss. "Saved by the bell."

It was, Laine decided, the most blissful day she could ever recall — and the most tactile. No matter where she and Drew were — on the beach, in the water, or on the boat — they couldn't seem to refrain from touching each other for very long. They were never more than a light kiss, a gentle stroke, a handhold apart.

Once, Drew caught her underwater. Pulling her hard against him, he'd welded his mouth to hers while flashes of brilliantly colored tropical fish swirled about them. Legs moving fluidly in synchronization, he stroked her from breast to thigh while they glided slowly to the surface for air.

Another time, he had insisted on applying suntan lotion to her arms and legs. Gently he'd eased her onto her stomach, the cool brush of his fingers soft as butterfly's wings as he slid first one narrow strap from her shoulder, then the other. He'd warmed the lotion in the palms of his hands, then proceeded to drive her into madness as he touched every inch of exposed skin on her body. His hands had stroked and tuned her flesh like a master violinist preparing for a concert. Having glided down her spine to massage her hips and explore her thighs with his magic touch, he'd then moved back up to her ribcage, where his thumbs repeatedly brushed her breasts.

Her body was part ice, part flame, as passion raced through her. And when she'd thought she would cry out with arousal, he'd stopped and reversed their positions. She became the tormentor, touching his body as he'd touched hers until at last Drew informed her in a broken whisper that he was dying by degrees and would she please go for a swim — so he could cool off.

The memory of their day still glowed as warm as the sunset embrace of the tropics when they stepped onto the dock at

Cancún in the dusky approach of evening. As had been the case since morning, they were touching, his arm draped loosely over her shoulders. The marina was a flurry of departing tourists, weary but content from a pleasant outing in the sun.

At first Laine paid little notice to the brown-skinned boy who sidled up to Drew and began to speak in low tones. Only when she felt Drew's body stiffen and grow tense did she give the child more than cursory attention. A soiled cotton shirt displaying the embroidery so popular in Mexico hung open to the waist. The shoeless lad looked to be about nine or ten and appeared to be trying to sell something.

"Go home." Drew's voice was tight and controlled.

"The *señor* will be pleased with my merchandise," the boy insisted, grinning up into the tall American's face.

"No."

"Is very good quality, from Colombia, *señor*."

Laine almost lost her balance when Drew skidded to a halt and turned on the boy. Bending down, he grabbed him by the arm and yanked him so their faces were only inches apart. A muscle jumped in Drew's jaw.

"If I thought it would do any good I'd haul you off to the nearest police station. It won't, so take your merchandise and get off the dock. And don't let me see you approach anybody else or I'll make good my threat. Now —" he spun the boy around and gave him a resounding whack on his rump "— *vamos.*"

"*Sí, sí,*" the frightened lad stammered, struggling to back away from the angry gringo.

Alternately stunned and alarmed as she witnessed the encounter, Laine realized with a jolt that she'd been watching two strangers. This angry, ominous Drew was a stranger too; formidable and terrifying. His face was a hard mask of intolerance, even loathing, and Laine was struck with the sobering thought

119

that she actually knew very little about the man to whom she had given her heart. Was it possible there was a dark side to Drew? Could her heart's choice have been a wrong one?

The stranger in question turned toward her, his face hardened with fury, his eyes cold, dull and distant as though he were reliving another such bitter moment in his life.

Drew gritted his teeth as a shudder ripped through his body and he struggled to subdue his anger. How many times would he have to remember the kids in Nam — from the very young, like the boy to teenagers who had just approached him, peddling drugs to GI's? How often could he fight the reminders of his impotent rage upon discovering one of his own men had been supplying those drugs? Dammit to hell, would that episode in his life forever haunt him?

"Drew?" Laine's voice seemed to call to him from far away. "Drew?"

His eyes lost their coldness and he gave his head a shake as if to clear it. "Laine?"

"Drew, are you all right? What — ?"

"Yeah, I'm fine," he interrupted, taking a deep breath before closing the distance between, physically and mentally. He gathered her to his side and gave her waist a squeeze. She was looking at him quizzically, but there was nothing in her eyes to indicate she had been repelled by his hellish trip down memory lane.

"You frightened me," she said quietly.

He stopped walking and pulled her into his arms, relishing the heat of her body, reveling in the warmth of her spirit. She was so precious he couldn't bear the thought of any ugliness touching her, particularly the kind he'd known in the past.

"Oh, Laine, I'm sorry. That's the last thing I ever want to do."

"It's okay." She reached up and smoothed a lock of hair

from his forehead in loving concern. "Drew, there's a lot I don't know about you, about your past. But one thing I do know, you're a gentle man. Anything that could arouse so much anger in you must be very important. Important enough to take you away from me for a even a moment." She smiled sweetly, hoping to erase the worried frown on his face.

"Nothing in this life or the next is that important." He kissed her sweet smile.

She wanted to believe him. This was her Drew talking, not the dark stranger of a moment ago. But a kernel of doubt had implanted itself in Laine's subconscious.

The sun was hanging low in the sky by the time they returned to the hotel. They both agreed to an early dinner, but thirty minutes after Laine had showered and changed for dinner, Drew hadn't arrived. She rang his room and got no answer, waited a few more minutes, then decided to look for him. As she hurried across the breezeway that connected the main part of the hotel with the guest rooms, she glanced beachward. Drew was standing not far from the water's edge, hands in his pockets, staring out to sea.

Beneath Drew's fixed gaze, waves rolled endlessly toward the shore. His distinguished face was brooding; the tensing of his jaw betrayed his deep frustration. *Damn that kid!* he silently cursed. But it was self-recrimination, not anger at the boy, that caused his current black humor. The misguided youngster was only a reminder of a past he wanted to forget — one he had no desire to relive or even share in recollection. A past that was definitely affecting his future. After years of forcing himself to avoid sharing anything with anyone, he was now faced with knowing he had to share his past with Laine. Should he tell her everything, including the most recent episode? Surely nothing from either of their pasts would change the way they felt

121

about each other. Or would it?

Drew's sigh was carried away on the evening breezes. He wasn't worried about her past, but he was sure as hell afraid of his. Would she look at him differently when he told her tales of his "colorful" life?

Would the fact that he'd lived by his wits and done whatever was required — even resorting to violence in the name of national security — appall her? He knew only two things: she trusted him, and he couldn't live without her. And if opening up a few old wounds could prove that what they had was in a class by itself, then he'd gladly bleed a little.

"Any man who would deliberately deprive himself of the company of an intelligent, beautiful, sexy woman in favor of a view needs some help," Laine teased lightly as she trudged through the warm sand to where he stood.

Drew's head whipped around and he quickly masked the startled expression on his face. Laine stood a few feet behind him, smiling, radiant in a silk halter dress that moved against her skin caressingly as she stepped closer. God, she was breathtaking with the colors of the sunset washing her complexion with gold.

"All I need is you." He drew her to him, lifting her off the sand in a bear hug. One of her sandals dropped with a soft plop and she laughed.

"You've swept me off my feet."

"Why, so I have. Shall I carry you off to my castle and ravish you?" He picked up the light tone of her mood, grateful that she hadn't mentioned his somber preoccupation.

"Sounds like lots of good clean fun, but you'll have to feed me first," she informed him between kisses. "Now, put me down and behave yourself."

"Killjoy."

"Sir, you wound me. I have only your best interest at heart," she said, thickly applying her Southern drawl.

"Oh yeah?"

"Yeah. Ravish me now, you'd never be sure if the growls you hear are coming from —" she dropped her voice seductively "— deep in my throat —" her voice returned to normal, if not a notch higher "— or my stomach."

Still holding her within the circle of his arms, he threw back his head and laughed out loud. The deep, warm, rich sound thrilled Laine and pushed her earlier doubts to the far corners of her mind.

"All right, you little pragmatist, but I'd better hear some pretty convincing growls before this night is over." He deposited her on the sand, kissed her swiftly, retrieved her shoe and gave her a gentle shove back up the beach to the hotel.

Dinner was delicious, although several times during the meal Laine noticed Drew seemed distracted. As the evening progressed, his reserve disturbed her, nourishing the seed of doubt. Their mutual unease began to erect an invisible wall between them. By the time they reached his room a couple of hours later, Laine's discomfort had grown into full-fledged anxiety.

In the short time they'd been together, Laine had experienced a kind of closeness she'd never known existed. Once exposed, she was loathe to forfeit the treasured connection, even if bold steps were required to recapture it. Her newfound security made her bold. She was determined to tear down the barriers and regain the sweet intimacy.

Immediately upon entering the room, Drew shrugged off his sport coat and heaved a heavy sigh as he turned from her.

"Maybe this wasn't such a good idea." She spoke quietly, awaiting his reaction with bated breath.

"No!" Two rapid strides brought him to her side, but he stopped short of reaching for her. "It was —" he placed one hand on his lean hip and raked his hair with the other "— is,

123

a terrific idea. I just . . ." His hesitation caused a knot of dread to form in the pit of her stomach.

"Drew, what's wrong? All through dinner I could feel you slipping away, closing yourself off. Don't you see?" She ached to reassure him that nothing would change her feelings, but her own doubts still nagged her. "We have to talk about whatever is bothering you . . . bothering us." Even to her own ears her voice sounded desperate. "It has something to do with the boy on the dock today, doesn't it?"

For a moment he studied her. "It wasn't just the boy, but how I reacted this afternoon. You're right. I shut you out deliberately." He turned soulful eyes on her. "I was afraid to let you get too close."

His heart-wrenching proclamation was a tiny ray of light as the door to his soul began to open. "Tell me." Her hand reached for his and their fingers entwined.

"I need to hold you while we talk. I need to feel you close to me." He scooped her into his arms and strode across the room. Gently, like placing a crown jewel on a velvet cushion, he lowered her to the bed and slipped down beside her, enfolding her in his embrace. His breath fanned the curls at her temple.

"You asked me once how long I'd been a federal prosecutor and I told you, since I left the service. I deliberately let you think I meant the military and in a way, I didn't lie. I was in Vietnam. Special Services. Do you know what that means?"

"Like Green Berets?" she questioned in a small voice.

"Something like that, only after the war I stayed with it. At one time or another I've worked cases on murderers, drug dealers, spies, every kind of trash known to the human race. And because of my work, I was a loner. Hell, what am I saying? I chose to be alone."

"But not anymore?"

"No, when I decided to leave the service and put my law degree to good use, I also decided to change that part of my life. It's been almost two years and I thought I'd overcome all my hang-ups about not sharing anything personal except what was needed in my work."

"You . . . you seem to," Laine insisted breathlessly.

"I thought so too, until you came along. Then I found out just how closely guarded I've kept myself. Laine, I spent years isolating myself emotionally for fear of being vulnerable. With you I was afraid that if I revealed my past, you would be frightened and pull away. Either way, I would lose."

Arching her back, she tilted her chin until she could look into his eyes. "You were afraid that your past, what you did for a living, would frighten me and I would turn away from you?"

He nodded.

"You couldn't be more wrong, Drew."

"Am I?"

"Yes." Compassion was mixed with a touch of exasperation. Why did she have to prove her trust? Wasn't the time they'd spent together proof enough? Realization flashed through her mind.

"Drew?" She touched his cheek and his lips moved instantly to her palm. "You've shared with someone before and been hurt, haven't you?"

Gently lifting her hand, he slowly moved her fingers back and forth across his lips as he spoke. "No — at least not the way you mean. I won't pretend there haven't been other women, but not a special woman. I learned very quickly that family, friends and particularly bedmates were definitely put off by my occupation. My line of work was a reminder of the seamier side of life. Watching it on the six o'clock news is one thing. To hear about it firsthand is quite another."

125

Her hand stilled its stroking. "And so you protected your-self."

He gazed down at her with an expression that was half pain, half joy. He nodded. "I didn't stop to think that what I'd done would backfire. I built a wall no one could scale, including me. Until I met you, I had locked myself inside, created a splendid isolation." He moved her delicate hand to his cheek and covered it with his.

Splendid isolation. The words rang with dazzling clarity. They were both guilty of secluding themselves from the real caring. Laine saw how she, too, had isolated herself and how, without even realizing it, she had willingly cast off her aloneness to be with him.

"Drew, I can't promise not to be shocked, maybe even horrified by what you say. I'm only human and I have a feeling you've been to hell a few times, but I won't turn away. I couldn't."

So, he told her. As much as he dared, as much as he thought she could handle. He told her about Vietnam, Beirut, Athens, even Moscow — of many of the places and events that had helped form the man he was.

She listened, and before he stopped talking her face was bathed with tears. Not just because he'd experienced the tor-tures of the damned, but because she hadn't been there waiting for him, to hold him and love him. As she listened, a clear picture of a man of pride and determination emerged. One who put duty before all else, one who had placed such a high value on honor and human rights that he'd sacrificed a part of himself to preserve them. She was filled to over-flowing with awe and love for this extraordinary man.

"I wish I'd been with you," she whispered, her voice break-ing with emotion.

"And been part of a nightmare, waiting to soothe the weary

warrior and watch him return to battle again?" He shook his head sadly. "I could never have done that to you."

Tears glistened on her pale cheeks like diamonds on satin, and Drew knew that if he lived to be a hundred he would never see anything as breathtakingly lovely as her face at that moment. With infinite tenderness he kissed her damp cheeks.

"My heart aches to think of you alone," Laine whispered softly.

"I don't feel alone anymore."

"You won't ever be again," she murmured hoarsely, the words forming a silken web of commitment in the quiet room.

His mouth became more seductive, drugging her senses, searing her flesh; and they flowed together like warm honey, the rich sweet nectar of desire swirling through their bodies.

He undressed her slowly, worshipfully, praising her body with soft kisses as he went. Deft fingers lifted her hair and released the halter tie. The silk bodice of her sundress whispered downward over her warm flesh. His mouth followed in heated pursuit, kissing the slender column of her throat, the soft swell of her breasts. His lips brushed her nipples, tantalizing them into rosy peaks. He strung kisses over her satiny skin, each one bringing her closer and closer to heaven.

He pushed the dress over her hips, sliding a hand beneath her, lifting, coaxing, until the smooth silk slithered over her legs and onto the floor. The last scrap of undergarment shielding her femininity followed the sensuous path of the dress. Drew lowered his head and placed a fervent kiss on the creamy skin of her stomach. Laine moaned his name again and again in a litany of mounting desire.

He separated from her only long enough to eliminate the barrier of his clothing, returning as gloriously naked as she. "You are exquisite." He mouthed the compliment against the velvety plane of her stomach, his tongue symbolically probing her navel. "I want to taste every inch of you. You fill me up, yet I can't get enough of you. I want to consume you until we move as one, love as one."

"Yes, yes," she cried, as he took that first step toward the oneness they both craved. She arched her back and rose to meet him.

Above her, his eyes blazed blue fire, while his hands caressed her throbbing breasts, thumbs petting the buds until she thought she would perish from the ache of wanting. His tongue painted slick circles around the tips. His lips enfolded a tender aureole and when he gently began to suckle, her body ceased to belong to her. He had stolen it completely.

"So good . . . You . . . feel so . . . I want . . ."

At her encouragement he increased the tempo of love, stoking the raging inferno within, driving her ever closer to the mind-shattering madness. Her fingernails dug into his buttocks as she climbed higher and higher on the ladder to the stars.

"Yes, tell me. Tell me what you want," he demanded in a raspy voice. "Do you want this —" he retreated almost to the point of withdrawal, but not quite, still moving with agonizing precision "— or this?" He plunged deep into her nectarous warmth.

"Ah . . . that's . . . yes, yes," she cried out as at last she entered the sweet explosion.

Drew shuddered as his own fulfillment fused with hers, and the glowing embers of their union endured long after the last tremor had echoed into quiet stillness. Moonlight sifted across the bed as they lay replete and content, their bodies lovingly entwined.

"I feel so . . . so . . ." His voice trailed off and his gaze searched hers.

"What?"

"Good." His answer seemed to surprise him.

Laine smiled. "Well, so do I."

"No, I mean *good*." His hand caressed her bare shoulder as he spoke. "Damn, I'm lousy at expressing myself. What I'm trying to say is I feel good inside. Like I'm new again; all bright, clean, fresh. I want to be everything for you. I want to give you everything, hand you the world on a silver platter."

"I don't want the world." *Your love will do,* she thought, as trembling fingers stroked a wayward golden curl from his forehead.

"Do you have any idea how completely you've changed my life?" His lips touching hers preempted her answer. The tender kiss lasted for long, delicious moments. Drew pulled back and gazed lovingly at her beautiful face. He paused, his blue eyes sparked with some indefinable emotion, then gave an infinitesimal nod as though having reached a decision.

Without warning, he slipped out of bed and bent from the waist, a forefinger snagging his discarded cutoffs. One hand disappeared into a pocket to curl around a small metal object.

Drew's movements were so fluid and rapid, Laine barely had time to question his departure before he was once again stretched on his side facing her. With a possessive familiarity granted only to lovers, his knee slid across her thighs and stayed. His hand, forming a relaxed fist, rested on the velvet of her abdomen. His other arm now rested between his head and the pillow, the point of his elbow gently touching the slope of her shoulder. Laine nuzzled his arm and across the pillow their gazes locked and held.

"Once, in Nam, I wound up with my own rifle stuck in my face and a Vietcong on the other end."

Wide-eyed, Laine sucked in her breath.

"My M-16 misfired. Probably the only time in my military career I forgot to clean my weapon." He closed his eyes tightly, then reopened them. "Anyway, I kept . . . the shell. Sounds

129

crazy, but I figured it had my name on it. My good-luck piece. As long as *I* had the cartridge, my life was safe."

He raised himself up on his elbow and opened the hand resting on her stomach to reveal a cylindrical-shaped metal object. Moonlight twinkled off the polished brass of a rifle bullet.

At her questioning look, he again enfolded the cartridge, brought the closed fist to his lips and very gently blew into the center. Still watching her face, he tenderly laid the cylinder, warmed by his breath, in the valley between her breasts. Instinctively her hand reached to cover the cartridge. His hand quickly covered hers.

"I trust you with my life."

The trajectory of his words was sure and true. As if his lucky charm had penetrated her flesh, his softly spoken pronouncement pierced her soul and embedded itself forever in her heart.

Moved beyond mere words, Laine blinked back tears of joy as she slipped her free hand behind his head and brought his lips to hers. If their joining had been sweet before, then love's encore was ecstasy almost beyond bearing. They fused together, reformed, and emerged as one.

A glorious pink dawn found the lovers awaking slowly, their bodies still intimately entangled.

"Are you nibbling on my arm?"

"Breakfast in bed," he murmured as his mouth and teeth made naughty little forays from her wrist to her shoulder.

"What about me?"

Without interrupting his preoccupation with her soft flesh, he glanced sideways and offered his forearm in response.

"No thanks, I prefer toast and coffee."

"Funny, last night I could have sworn you showed a decided taste for human flesh — mine."

"How ungentlemanly of you to remind me of my baser instincts so early in the morning."

"Hmm, but what a nice way to begin the day."

The sensuous journey ended with his tongue tracing the outline of her ear.

"Ah . . . I . . . did you . . . have something special planned for today?"

He drew back to look at her, working his eyebrows up and down in a lecherous manner.

"Stop that, you oversexed . . ."

"Madam, I am the soul of propriety."

"You're the soul of wickedness, and if you don't stop leaving teeth marks all over my —"

He took a love bite of the soft fullness of one breast, bringing a gasp to her lips.

"Does this mean breakfast will be delayed?" Her breathing became accelerated.

"Indefinitely."

"Will you make it up to me?"

"Absolutely."

"When?"

"Now."

Not only thoughts of breakfast, but of lunch as well, took second place to the hunger they shared, a hunger abated only by feasting on love.

Chapter 9

Laine had the eerie feeling that she was being watched. Instinctively her gaze drifted casually over the other occupants of the hotel lobby. Drew was buying a U.S. newspaper at the desk, bellboys scurried back and forth with their burdens amid the excited conversations of new arrivals, and staff trafficked through the lobby going about their normal business. Nothing appeared out of the ordinary; still, the feeling persisted.

"Pardon me," Drew's deep voice came from directly behind her right shoulder, "but can you tell me where I might find an agreeable, intelligent, attractive woman interested in investigating the local beaches with me — object: relaxation and pleasant conversation?"

"Is this a pickup?"

"I'm giving it my best shot."

"Do you fool around?"

"Hell no, lady. I'm dead serious." He laughed and planted a light kiss on the tip of her nose. "Miss me?"

"Desperately." She smiled at him.

"I was beginning to wonder. You looked like you were checking over alternates as I walked up."

"Guilty." She sighed theatrically. "But a poor crop. Guess I'll just have to settle for what I've got."

"I'll try not to disappoint you."

"You haven't." Her voice dropped almost a full octave and she gave him a longing, promise-filled look.

Drew could hardly restrain himself from dragging her back upstairs to exact delicious payment. One smoldering look from her and his brain turned to oatmeal, all else promptly forgotten except his overwhelming desire for her.

"Tell me again precisely what you wanted to do with the rest of the day?" he inquired huskily.

"To go to the beach?"

"Ah, yes, the beach. Warm sand, gentle surf caressing cool bodies . . ."

"Stop that," Laine said with a laugh.

"Stop what?"

"You know what."

"Completely?"

"Temporarily."

"All right, postponement granted. Now let's get going before I have to throw myself on the mercy of the court." Arms around each other's waists, they started for their rooms to change into swimsuits.

Out of the corner of his eye, a figure caught Drew's attention. With calculated indifference he turned his head. At the same time, the man lifted his eyes and met Drew's gaze. An imperceptible nod acknowledged the eye contact.

"Damn," Drew muttered under his breath.

"What?" Laine looked up in surprise as Drew came to a halt.

"I, uh, suntan lotion." He snapped his fingers. "Do we need more lotion?"

"We used it all yesterday. Remember?" She gave him a knowing smile.

"Vividly. That's why we need more. I'd hate to pass up the opportunity to, ah, repeat yesterday's delightful experience. Why don't you go to the gift shop and pick some up."

"Aren't you coming with me?" Laine felt strangely reluctant to leave him.

"I know you can't bear to be parted from my gorgeous body —" he pulled a smug face and continued his teasing, but his eyes didn't reflect the jovial tone "— but, wonderful person that I am, I noticed the serving hut on the beach closes during siesta. So, with my usual attention to your every comfort —" he made a lopsided bow from the waist "— I'm going to order two glasses of something cool for us to pick up after we've changed. Can you manage without me?"

"I'll do my best, but . . ." Her teasing comeback faded into silence as he raised her hand to his lips and placed a warm kiss in her palm, followed by a flick of his tongue.

She sighed, then wrinkled her nose and kissed the air in his direction. "You'd better not keep me waiting," she said softly as she turned to go.

Walking away, an uncanny feeling of fear engulfed her. A glance over her shoulder revealed Drew watching her from across the foyer. He was smiling, but in a detached sort of way. Somehow she knew his thoughts were far removed from suntan lotion and her.

As soon as Laine disappeared from view, Drew whirled and headed straight for the man he'd recognized — Agent Lyle Dunning.

"What the hell are you doing here?" Drew glanced uneasily over his shoulder, then back to the agent.

"Wakefield's dead."

"Dead? When? How?"

"His car exploded last night."

"I'm sorry." The regret in Drew's voice was genuine. Ron Wakefield was definitely one of the good guys.

"J. R. wants you back in the office."

Drew's eyes narrowed. "Why?"

Dunning shot him a hard look. "I told you, Wakefield's no longer available."

"Neither am I." Drew bit out the words. "What about Elroy?"

"No good. The only means of identification went up in

134

smoke with Wakefield. J. R. thinks we've got quite a conversationalist in our little group. Besides, he's worried you might follow Wakefield, since you're the only person alive who can ID Barlow."

"Not likely. That's not Barlow's style."

"That's not the story we get, and Rankin doesn't want to take any chances."

"Where is Rankin?"

Dunning shrugged. "Washington, I guess. Why?"

"I tried to reach him yesterday. A guy was following me."

"Did you get a good look at him?"

"Yeah, but he got away before I could find out who contracted his services."

"Describe him. I'll see what we can come up with."

"Mexican national. Black hair. Mustache. About five-foot-ten."

"That's not much to go on."

"Sorry, it's the best I can do."

"Time is short, Kenyon. I'm here to escort you to the airport. There's a plane standing by."

"I'm not alone."

"Yes, but it can't be helped."

A pulsing knot of frustration coiled into a tight ball in the pit of Drew's stomach. Wakefield had been a good man. The agency had to nail Barlow and put him away for keeps. There was no choice. Would Laine understand?

"All right." Drew's sigh of resignation belied the tension as his hands rolled into fists and the muscles in his neck became rigid. "Give me an hour to make my excuses."

For the first time since he'd first spoken to Kenyon, Lyle Dunning was uneasy. For a routine fetch-and-carry operation, the scenario was turning out to be very complicated. It was even more difficult because he knew Kenyon was on vacation

135

— and with a very good-looking woman. Dunning's features softened, understanding Drew's dilemma. "No can do."

"You mean, leave now?" Rancor sharpened Drew's voice. "I can't just —"

"Look —" the agent's voice turned deliberately cold and lashing "— I've got my orders and they don't include your lady friend. My job is to baby-sit you until I hand you over to another 'nanny' at the Cancún airport. After that, it's somebody else's responsibility to make sure you stay in one piece. Use your head, Kenyon; we can't run the risk of someone trying to get to you through her. If she comes along, her head's on the block right alongside yours." He let his words sink in.

Drew saw the stony resolve in the other man's face and knew Dunning was right. If anything happened to Laine because of him . . . No, he couldn't take that chance.

"My luggage?"

"Taken care of along with the bill."

"Your generosity overwhelms me."

"It's on the company."

"Remind me to write my congressman a thank-you note," Drew sniped as he snatched a quick look over his shoulder at Laine standing at the checkout counter in the gift shop. Thank goodness her back was to him. He wouldn't be able to smile and wave with any sincerity if she looked his way.

Laine tapped the side of the bottle of suntan oil against the heel of her hand, waiting for the customer ahead of her to make her purchase. The notion that Drew was somehow not himself nagged at her. Concern compelled her to glance through the glass windows separating the shop from the lobby. Drew was still there, but he wasn't talking to a waiter. Her attention went to the man speaking with Drew. He wore wrinkled khaki slacks, a faded tropical-print shirt and an angry frown. Even though she couldn't see Drew's face, his body

136

language spoke volumes. He faced the stranger with clenched fists and rigid shoulders. She froze as the man's hand closed over Drew's arm.

Laine tilted her head to one side and frowned. Her previous doubts began to mushroom into full-blown fears. Who was with Drew?

She watched the ill-sorted pair walk across the lobby and through the hotel entrance toward a waiting vehicle. Not until they reached the car did the stranger release his hold on Drew's arm.

Where were they going? Why didn't Drew wait for her? He wouldn't simply go off without a word . . . Icy fingers of apprehension shot down Laine's spine. *Unless he had no choice.*

Frantic, Laine raced from the boutique, tossing the unpaid-for plastic tube of sunscreen on a nearby stack of beach towels. By the time she reached the revolving glass door at the entrance, the car, the stranger and Drew were nowhere to be seen.

Nervous perspiration dotted her upper lip, her heart was hammering and logic sifted away from her grasp like sand through an hourglass. Irrational fears crowded the dark corners of her mind. Vivid word pictures evoked by Drew's tales of his past streaked through her memory. The people, places and events, which at the time had sounded to Laine like pages from a Ludlum novel — nightmarish adventures — she now saw from a different perspective. Was Drew's disappearing act somehow connected to his past life? She shivered, not from the chill of the semi-airconditioned lobby, but from fearful reality.

But he would have told her he was leaving, she reasoned. *If he could,* that same reason reminded her, *if he could.*

Abducted! The word blazed through her mind. *No! Not in broad daylight . . . yet, the stranger did seem to be in charge of the situation . . . of Drew.* The blood pounded in Laine's temples until it made a deafening roar. A frightening certainty settled upon her. She must do something! With a heavy heart she walked toward the front desk.

The clerk behind the reservations desk smiled politely as Laine approached. *"Buenas tardes."*

"My name is Laine Stewart, room 207. I . . . did Mr. Kenyon leave a message for me?"

"I will see. One moment, please." He returned seconds later. "I am sorry, no message."

In her agitated state she'd forgotten that Drew's room had become their room. "Will you check Mr. Kenyon's room, 421, just in case . . ."

"Yes, just a moment, please." The clerk disappeared again. "I'm sorry." The pleasant young man smiled an apology as he reemerged. "But there was nothing."

"Thank you." Laine turned away, then stopped and faced the clerk again. "Can you tell me when Mr. Kenyon will return?"

"Sí." He flipped through a file directly in front of him until he located the card he sought. *"Perdoneme.* He has checked out of the hotel."

"I don't . . . don't understand."

"Another gentleman, a business associate, I believe he said he was, checked Mr. Kenyon out early this morning. He told me Mr. Kenyon was going home today." The clerk's enigmatic words didn't help the drumming in Laine's head.

"Home?"

"Sí." His voice softened in sympathy. "The man brought Mr. Kenyon's luggage down to the lobby and paid the bill. Is there anything else I can do for you, *señorita?"*

"No . . . no, thank you," Laine whispered, her throat tightening around the words.

Dazed, she turned away from the helpful clerk. Outwardly, she was very still; inside, her body trembled uncontrollably.

Someone else had checked Drew out of the hotel. Was that "someone" the stranger who left with Drew? Where did they go, and why? None of it made any sense, except for the one suspicion her befuddled mind seemed to center on again and again. *All of the events of the morning must be related to Drew's past as an agent of the United States government.* Laine wasn't sure exactly what the connection was; that much of the puzzle still eluded her. She refused to consider any other logical reason for Drew's behavior. For a fleeting moment, the deep-seated, hidden fear surfaced to offer an alternative reason. Old fears crowded her head. Was he using her?

Not once had he mentioned love. Need, yes; but not love. Love words had been whispered and loving gesture exchanged, but Drew had never spoken the three potent words.

Must the words be spoken to be felt?

Yes. She was no different from any other woman who longed to hear a whispered "I love you" across a candlelit table or a pillow. The words were important. Then why hadn't she spoken them to Drew? Because if saying the words was risky, the feelings behind them were terrifying. Maybe Drew was reluctant to speak for similar reasons.

Or, perhaps he simply made it a point to end relationships just short of the momentous commitment.

She didn't want to think about the last possibility. It was too painful. No. She fought to reject her suspicions and a suffocating sense of panic. *This can't be happening. It's some kind of crazy nightmare.* But there was no denying he'd gone, and without so much as a good-bye.

Gone! The single word bespoke the turmoil of her emotions. Tears gathered on her lower lashes as she placed a shaking hand to her mouth. "Gone," she whispered against icy-cold fingers as she gazed through the glass doors of the hotel to the spot where the car had been.

139

* * * * *

The car in question was racing toward the Cancún airport. With each mile, Drew's anger and frustration grew. Damned if Rankin hadn't called the tune and he'd danced! Self-righteous anger welled inside Drew from simmer to boiling point. *Where the hell does Rankin get off, pulling a cloak-and-dagger stunt like this!* The agent beside him hadn't uttered a word since the car sped away from the hotel. Drew now turned his anger full force on the nearest available target.

"Dammit! Who do you think you are, yanking me out of that hotel at the drop of a hat?" His face was a glowering mask of fury. "Why the bum's rush? Another half hour wouldn't have mattered."

"My orders stated 'without delay.' I told you, J. R. thinks your life might be in danger."

"Just like that!" Drew spat belligerently.

"Just like that," Dunning returned sharply. "You want us to put someone else's life on the line to nab Barlow?"

"What about my life!"

"Yours was on the line from the minute you testified at Barlow's court martial. You've been on his hit list for years." The angry retort hardened Dunning's already stony features.

Drew glared at the man, knowing he spoke the truth and hating him for it.

But Drew's *life* was back in that hotel. "Dammit, man. I can't just leave like this. I'm going to call Laine from the airport. I've got to tell her . . . something."

"You know it's against company policy."

Drew indicated in very precise expletives what the "company" could do with their policies, then leaned over the front seat, demanded and received a pencil and a piece of paper from the driver. He scribbled something down, then folded the note in half.

140

"Will you get this to her?"

Dunning looked at the note, then back at Drew. "You're pushing it, Kenyon."

"Then I might as well go all the way. Either you see she gets this or I don't go. I mean it."

The threat was impotent, but the determined set of Drew's jaw gave it just enough credence that Dunning decided not to force the issue. If a lie would placate his charge and return him to reasonability, then so be it.

"All right, but if this ever gets out, both our butts will be grass under Rankin's lawn mower." He tucked the note securely into his pocket.

Minutes later, Drew was whisked aboard a jet bound for Washington, D.C. Dunning watched as the doors closed on Drew and the "nanny" assigned for the next leg of his journey. Unsmiling, the Cancún based agent withdrew the folded piece of paper from his pocket and briefly scanned the words scribbled on it.

The short, cryptic message, hastily scrawled in a bold handwriting read:

Laine, had to leave. Will be in touch soon as possible. I love you! D.

The last three words preceding his initial were underlined twice.

"Sorry, pal." Dunning crumpled the note, took a deep drag on his half-smoked cigarette, then ignited the wad of paper and dropped it to the ground. Before the jet's wheels cleared the runway, the ashy remains of Drew's message to Laine disappeared beneath the agent's grinding heel; then the tropical breeze carried the puff of powdery dust into the Cancún sunshine.

Fatigue hung like a heavy mantle around Drew's neck and shoulders as he entered John Rankin's office the next morning. It was still dark outside.

"Good morning."

"That's questionable," was Drew's clipped response.

Rankin observed Drew closely. There was a tinge of grayness visible even beneath the newly acquired tan, and several new finely-etched lines had appeared around his mouth and eyes. He looked more haggard than when last they spoke, but it was understandable.

"John, can we dispense with the preliminaries and get on with it?"

"All right." Rankin sighed, pushed his chair back from the desk, propped both elbows on the padded arms and interlocked his fingers in front of his chest. "You know about Wakefield?"

"Dunning told me. Damn them! Ron was a good man."

In the silence that followed, Rankin swung his chair around to stare out the window at the Washington skyline. "When his car exploded, I was close by, but there was nothing anyone could have done." A thread of recrimination laced his scratchy voice.

"And the tape?"

"Wakefield had it with him. It was our only copy."

"But that's not possible!" Drew objected vehemently. "Records *never* let material out of their hands without making sure at least one copy exists. He couldn't have taken the tape out of here without approval. Who in the hell is responsible for such a monumental screwup?"

Rankin's body went rigid. He whipped the chair back to face Drew, his dangerously unyielding countenance reflecting an inner rage and frustration. "The guilty party is paying dearly, I can assure you."

"You're positive Barlow was behind the bombing?"

"Is there any doubt?"

"Then the man in Cancún was probably one of Barlow's henchmen."

"Probably. I wish to hell you had been able to reach me earlier. The guy may have been a nobody, but he could have been a direct link to Barlow. If we'd been able to keep him from contacting his boss, maybe we *could* have found out who was selling information. There's a leak somewhere down the line. And if I ever get my hands on the double-dealing bastard playing both sides of the fence . . ." His voice trailed off and his hands formed knuckled fists on the worn arms of his chair.

Drew remained silent, watching Rankin struggle, then emerge victorious over his temporary loss of control.

"If there had been another way to handle the situation, you wouldn't be here." John was once again in command, his voice cool, level. "We know Barlow is selling to Libya. You know his contact. The only thing we're unsure of is the exact time and place. It has to be soon, within the next week to ten days. But all the plans have been changed. Originally, a six-man team was set up; now we've cut it back to three. The fewer who know, the less chance of a double cross. The Reese people have been told as little as possible and I want it to stay that way. Even the team of agents won't know all the details until the last minute."

"Who're the others?"

Rankin shook his head. "We're operating on a strict need-to-know basis. When we get closer to D day, you'll have names."

"I take it you're the only one with all the pieces to the puzzle?"

"There's one other, but no cause for concern. It's safer that

143

way. In the meantime, go back to your apartment, work, do whatever you normally do. Just don't do it where we can't keep an eye on you."

"Does that mean —"

"It means," Rankin interrupted, "no unnecessary contact with *anybody*. We stand a good chance of nailing Barlow once and for all and getting a mammoth chunk of Khadafy's blood money in the bargain. This time nothing is going to go wrong, or by God, some heads are going to roll and some butts are going to be kicked. Do I make myself clear?"

"As a bell."

Rankin stood up, bent to a stack of papers and began flipping through them. Drew stared at the thinning patch of hair atop Rankin's head and knew he had been dismissed. Orders had been delivered and received — the interview was over. Drew had a job to do, one he couldn't forsake. Not even for love could he shirk his responsibility.

"When will I leave for Texas?"

"You'll be notified."

Drew rose to his feet and was opening the office door when a voice he barely recognized as Rankin's stopped him.

"Wakefield's wid— the family ask— requested we send no flowers, but make a contribution to his favorite charity." Rankin lifted his head, his eyes over-bright as they met Drew's gaze. "The services will be tomorrow afternoon. Call my secretary, Mrs. Riley, in the morning; she has all the details. I wish I could give you permission to attend, but under the circumstances . . ."

With a silent nod of understanding, Drew left the room.

The sweltering Washington heat engulfed him as he exited his office building and ambled down the sidewalk. He had no destination in mind; he just needed to walk and think. Stopping at a street corner, he glanced back over his shoulder. Approximately fifty yards behind him, he spotted his assigned companion.

Me and my shadow, Drew thought sarcastically. The light changed and he strolled on, hands in his pockets.

Oh, Laine, what must you be thinking? That I've deserted you. If you only knew. But you don't and you can't.

Without realizing it, he headed in the direction of his apartment, covering the ground with a measured tread indicative of his mental effort to put some perspective back into the past week. But his concentration centered on only one thought: Laine, and how much he loved her. And how, in all likelihood, he had lost her.

When she discovered he'd left, had she ranted and raved, called him every vile name in the book? Had she cried? He wondered if she would be objective enough to link his vanishing act with all the things he'd told her about his past. After a few short days, could he expect her to realize he loved her more than life itself? He'd told her in the note, but would she believe him?

Futilely, he tried to put himself in her place. How would he react if the situation were reversed? Hurt. First he'd be hurt, then madder than a hornet's nest. Then, he would want to find out what happened, and why. He would go looking for her.

Please, God, don't let her get mixed up in this mess. I couldn't live with myself if even one hair on her head were harmed because of me.

If he could call her, see her. And touch her and . . . He cautioned himself against giving such longings free rein. God, but he loved her, needed her. Now, more than ever.

Drew stopped dead still in the middle of the busy sidewalk, listening to his last words ricochet off the walls of his mind. He needed her, more than ever. The loner was alone no more.

145

She had seeped into his mind and his heart until every breath he drew, every impulse in his brain, was filled with her. She shadowed his thoughts every waking hour. She haunted him; a lovely ghost, the spirit of his heart. Longing for the sound of her voice speared his insides like a burning arrow. He recalled her sweet face as they lay in each other's arms the night before, remembered her soft lips kissing him.

But a kiss remembered wasn't good enough.

Rankin's orders were "No *unnecessary* contact." But hearing Laine say she loved him was as necessary as breathing.

He checked to see if his shadow was still trailing behind, then ducked into a nearby restaurant and found a phone booth. His fingers trembled as he punched out the area code for Dallas.

Chapter 10

The Dallas skyline glittered like diamonds scattered on black velvet as the taxi bearing Laine to her apartment sped swiftly through the pre-dawn darkness. Normally, she found the view stunning and welcoming. This morning she barely noticed, her thoughts far removed from the city and its myriad lights. She longed to be in another place, the place where her heart dwelled . . . with Drew.

Where was that? Laine could only guess. She had played the guessing game from the moment she had realized he was gone. The questions refused to stop. The answers, similar to her feelings, were vague and unsatisfying. All the checking and leads Laine had unraveled in Cancún had led to a dead end. Still, she was unable to shake the feeling that his disappearance had something to do with his past.

Why hadn't Drew tried to reach her? Surely he had returned to the States by now. But where? Washington or some other godawful place, perhaps on the other side of the world? No matter how many times Laine tried to put the pieces of the puzzle together, she couldn't. Only Drew had the missing pieces, only he could give her the answers she sought. Maybe he was leading her down the garden path, but if she were being led astray, Laine wanted to hear it from him. Somehow, she knew, she *had* to find a way to get in touch with him.

Wearily, she trudged up the front walk to her condominium, the humid air clinging to her body, making her fatigue all the more acute. Exhausted, she leaned against the front door while digging into her handbag for the key.

The jangling of the telephone catapulted her into action

147

and she scrambled to open the door.

"Hello."

"Laine?"

The sound of his voice was pure, sweet adrenaline.

"Drew? Oh, Drew, where are you? What happened to you? Are you all right?"

"Yes, I'm fine. Much better now that I hear your voice."

"Oh, God, you don't know what's been going through my mind. I've been frantic with worry. Are you sure you're all right?"

A shudder of relief swept through Drew's body. No accusations. No hateful recriminations. Her concern for his welfare was music to his ears. Lord, what wonderful thing had he done in his life to deserve such a woman?

"Oh, Laine, Laine," he whispered fervently into the phone.

"What . . . what is it?"

"I hated leaving the way I did. If there had been any other way . . . Hurting you is the last thing I want to do. You must believe that."

"I do," she said quietly.

Laine heard his long tortured sigh and could almost feel the tension flow from his body.

"Drew?" She paused, not knowing which question to ask first.

"I'm in Washington," he began, as though he'd read her mind.

"Thank God," she murmured under her breath.

"What did you say?"

"I said 'Thank God.' I was afraid . . . When you left, I — my imagination went wild. For all I knew, you could have wound up in a ditch along some road. I was terrified, imagining all sorts of things. I wasn't sure if I'd ever hear from you again."

"Didn't you get my note?"

"What note?"

"You didn't receive a note saying I would get in touch with you?"

"No."

"Dammit to hell! I ought to kill Dunn—"

"Drew, stop it! You're scaring me to death. There was no note! What is going on?"

"Laine, I'm sorry. I can't tell you much for now. But, damn, you must have thought . . ." His voice trailed off and she heard him sigh again. "You have every right to be mad as hell."

He almost sounded as though he wanted her to be.

"I was, a little. Until I began to remember all you'd told me about your past. Then I became so frightened. At this moment, I'm more confused than anything else."

"I know. You have a million questions. Unfortunately, right now I can't give you any answers. I can only tell you not to worry. Everything is going to work out, I promise."

"What do you mean? What is there to 'work out'? Drew, can't you tell me something . . . anything?" She had a nagging suspicion that whatever his answer was, she wasn't going to like it.

"Laine, I've been reassigned to the Reese case."

His words landed like a blow to her midsection and she gasped for air.

"But . . . I don't understand. You told me you quit. What about the law practice in New Orleans? Are you giving it up? Can they just call you back at the drop of a hat?"

"I didn't have a choice. When I told you I had no responsibilities to the prosecutor's office, I meant it. At the time, I had no idea the man assigned to the case would be . . . unable to finish." He chose his words carefully, selecting the least frightening.

149

"Can't finish? Why? Isn't there anyone else who can take his place?"

"No."

A single word, no explanation, no elaboration; just a very final-sounding "no."

"I —" She wanted to question him further, but stopped herself. "Your reasons are your own." It was her turn to sigh.

"Sweet reason," he said.

"What?"

"Nothing," he said. "Just an outdated legal term an old law-school professor was fond of. It means 'good reason; the best reason.' "

"Oh," she replied absently. "Will you be returning for the next grand jury session?"

Across the miles, Drew heard in her voice the dread mixed with longing. Even if he were in Dallas, they couldn't be together. He raked his fingers through his hair and gritted his teeth. If worse came to worse, he would have to lie to her; and the thought went against his grain. But the less she knew, the less danger to her.

"I'm not sure when the next session is scheduled."

Well aware he had avoided answering her question, Laine chewed her bottom lip, fighting the feeling of abandonment she had despite her faith in him.

"Will you call me as soon as you know anything?"

"Yes."

"Can I . . . would it be all right if I called you?"

"I, uh, may not be able to receive your calls for a while." He eyed the confinement of the telephone booth and silently cursed Rankin and the whole U.S. government. Stretching the rules was one thing, flaunting the fact was another. If he wanted to talk to Laine, it would have to be quick and clandestine. "It's better if I call you."

"Will you?"

The anxiety so evident in her voice tore him apart. His fingers tightened on the receiver.

"As often as I can."

She wanted to scream "When? Every night? Every week? Never?" All her trust, all her love was tied up in a man who couldn't even guarantee her a phone call.

"Laine?" His voice caressed her as though he were just a touch away.

"Yes."

"I miss you. Last night was hell. I tossed and turned, reaching for you a hundred times. Without you, I'm incomplete."

She gave up fighting; the tears slid down her cheeks unchecked.

"Oh, Drew." When he spoke to her with that soft, deep voice, she was undone. "I miss you, too. I don't like waking up without you next to me."

"God," he whispered. "I keep remembering the way you looked, lying in bed, fresh from our loving. Your body all soft and warm, curled next to mine. We fit so perfectly together."

"Drew . . ." she begged, her fingers barely able to hang on to the phone. Her mouth was as dry as parchment and every inch of skin felt hot and cold, all at the same time.

"I know, I know. But I can't help myself. I want to be with you so badly I can taste it. And . . ." Across the miles she could almost hear him grinding his teeth, holding back his frustration. "And I'm not making it any easier on you, am I? Damn! I'm sorry, love." He gave a derisive snort. "All I've done is apologize since you said hello. And we're right back where we started: apart."

"Not quite. I love you."

The words slipped out as naturally as if she had been saying them all her life. She was mildly shocked, but relieved and suddenly very sure.

"Oh, Laine —"

"I didn't expect to feel the way I do. At first, I didn't even want to. I only know I can't stop. A thousand miles away, or lying next to me, I love you, and I'll go on loving, no matter what."

The strength of her love touched him like an electric current transmitted through endless miles of inanimate wire cable, connecting their minds and their hearts, reaching out, energizing him with new hope.

"I hope you always will."

A slow, agonizing silence drifted over the wires.

"Laine?"

"Yes." She waited, hoping.

"I . . . Will you be all right?"

As all right as she could be without the words she longed to hear. "For now."

"Close your eyes." He paused for a second, his own eyelids slipping down. "Can you visualize my face?"

"Yes."

A crystal-clear picture of her beloved visage swam before him. "Can you feel my lips touch yours?"

"Yes-s-s."

His lips trembled as the imaginary kiss inflamed him. "Think of me, my love."

Laine sat perfectly still for long minutes listening to the buzz of the dial tone, yet not really hearing its drone. Finally, regretfully, she replaced the receiver in the cradle of the telephone. A sob caught in her throat as she wrapped both her arms around her waist and rocked back and forth. "Goodbye, my love," she whispered into the silence.

The days following Drew's call, Laine decided, were the longest in her life. The hours seemed to drag into centuries, each day longer than the one before. She threw herself into her job but found no ease for her loneliness and restlessness. And every time the phone rang at work or at home, she practically jumped out of her skin before dashing to answer it. Friends calling to inquire about her trip were treated to a five-sentence travelogue or informed of a ghastly headache that prevented long conversations. But Drew didn't call again and Laine began to wonder if she might have dreamed their conversation. She had only to close her eyes and the memory of his words convinced her of its reality. She closed her eyes frequently.

Other than the intense ache of separation that grew each day, her life had quickly returned to the usual. Except for one extraordinary occurrence. As she left office for lunch on her first day back to work, the receptionist, affectionately referred to as "Buttons," stopped her.

"There was a guy in here about a half-hour ago asking after you."

"Did he leave a message?"

"Nope. Just came in and — Good afternoon, Continental," the girl announced in a singsong voice. "Would you hold, please? — He asked if you still worked here. I offered to buzz you, but he said 'Never' — I'll ring for you now, sir — Said he had another call and he would get back to you later. New boyfiend?" Fascinated, Laine watched the operator's fingers dance over the flashing lights of the switchboard.

"No. What did he look like?"

"I'm sorry, sir. That line is busy, would you care to hold? Thank you." Buttons frowned and tapped a clean, unpolished nail against her lower lip. "Kind of ordinary, if you ask me. I mean, Robert Redford he wasn't. You know, the usual; suit,

153

tie, two arms, two legs, a briefcase."

"That all?"

"Yeah. Maybe some vendor wanting to see you about the convention booths." Buttons shrugged her shoulders expressively. "But . . ."

"But what?"

"He had the cutest dimples I ever saw. When he smiled they just seemed to pop out, or would that be in? Anyway, he had Howdy Doody dimples. One moment, please, I'll transfer you."

"Thanks, I think," Laine said, smiling as she exited the reception area.

The unknown caller was promptly forgotten until later the same day. Eager not to miss a possible call from Drew, she made a mad dash through the supermarket for necessary items: coffee, toothpaste and frozen dinners. She didn't want to be in the middle of cooking if . . . when . . . Drew called. While she zipped down the aisles, a man, presumably just another shopper, strolled past her and smiled.

His dimples were definitely of the Howdy Doody variety.

A totally insane thought, but there it was, nonetheless. *You have lost it, lady! You're seeing agents behind every box of pancake mix!* At that precise moment, a small boy dashed past her waving a box of cereal and yelling "Daddy, Daddy!" Laine was greatly relieved to see familiar dimples on the chubby face. The incident, however, caused her to question any strange man.

On her way to work the next day, she was almost certain she saw one parked in a car at the end of her street. Uneasiness grew into full-fledged worry. As crazy as it sounded, she became convinced the man was watching her. There was no question in her mind that his surveillance had something to do with Drew, but what could she do? Go up and accost the man? Ask

154

if he was following her, and why? No, Laine cautioned herself; the direct approach was not the way to proceed. She would try to ignore his presence. She wouldn't go out of her way to avoid the man, but neither would she be content to be constantly under his watchful eye. Act normal, but keep a sharp lookout and wait, she finally decided.

At the end of the third day without any contact from Drew, Laine arrived home disheartened and depressed. She tossed her keys on the hall table, dropped down onto the sofa and began to shuffle through the day's mail, hoping against hope for some word from Drew. The plain white envelope bearing the address of the Dallas Federal Courthouse stamped in bold black in the upper left-hand corner stood out from the other pieces of mail like a basketball player at a Munchkins reunion.

A special session of the grand jury was to convene on Wednesday of the following week!

In a week, just a few short days, she would see Drew. Their being together outside the jury room no longer mattered. She didn't care that she would be granted only the brief hours between nine and five each day to see him, hear his voice. The fact that she would see him was the only thing that mattered. They would be together, if only in spirit. The idea of being so close, yet not close enough, was glorious agony, giving her cause to wonder just how strong she would be when the time arrived. In the final analysis it made no difference, because she would gladly submit to the tortures of the damned so long as she could see him again for even eight minutes, much less eight hours.

The digital clock showed Tuesday, 11:58 P.M., when the phone rang, jarring Laine from her half-awake state.

A single ring was barely completed before the receiver was next to her ear.

"Hello?"

"Did I wake you?"

The smooth, rich timbre of his voice flowed over and around her, sending adrenaline racing through her veins. She felt more alive than she had in days. Her skin began to tingle with warmth and her heartbeat paced a hummingbird's wings.

"I was waiting, hoping you would call. How are you?"

"Fine. And you?"

"Fine."

They both sounded so polite, so controlled. This isn't right, she thought. It isn't real.

"I lied," she amended quickly. "I'm not fine. I'm lonely."

"We both lied," he confessed, wishing it were the only lie she would hear from his lips. "I miss you like the devil."

"I'm glad. The only thing keeping me going is the knowledge I'll see you very soon."

"Me, too." He hated the lie he had to speak.

"When will you be here?"

"I should arrive in Texas sometime tomorrow." Would she catch the fact he said Texas, not Dallas?

"Tomorrow! Oh Drew, what time? In the morning? When?"

"I, uh, think my flight gets in shortly after noon."

"Oh. That means I won't see you until . . . day after tomorrow?"

The disappointment in her voice twisted like a knife in his gut. If only he could assure her that he would see her on Thursday, or any day for that matter. Lying to keep her safe was one thing, but making promises he couldn't guarantee was something he would not do to her. She deserved at least that much. Hell, she deserved a lot more than that.

"I'm as disappointed as you are, sweetheart, but it's out of my hands. 'Ours is not to reason why . . .' " *What an asinine thing to do, Kenyon. Of all lines to quote!*

"Yes, I know," she said, her voice distracted, distant.

Laine sounded as depressed as he felt. Drew didn't want

the conversation to end, but he knew the current topic had to be changed.

"What were you doing when I called?"

"Lying in bed, waiting for you to call."

"And were you thinking up dirty words to whisper in my ear? Careful. Ma Bell takes a dim view of that sort of thing."

"Ma Bell is my only true friend at this point. She'll understand and forgive. Besides, isn't she always telling us to reach out and touch someone?"

"Yes, but not there."

She couldn't help herself. He was trying so hard to lighten the mood, some of it was bound to spill onto her. A giggle erupted. "You're a pervert."

"True, true, but you love perverts."

"Must be my week for strange men," she rejoined.

"Oh, who else has been 'strange' with you?" The smile in his voice altered marginally.

"Nobody, really. My imagination is working overtime. I see weirdos lurking around the canned-goods section and on street corners."

"Where?"

"The grocery store, silly. The other day I thought some man was watching me in the supermarket and then again some man parked at the end of my street."

"Are you sure?" If Rankin had a man keeping an eye on her, Drew was relieved. But what if it wasn't one of Rankin's people? Drew's heart lurched at the thought.

"I'm sure I've gone more than a little paranoid. Must be these late-night calls from dirty old men."

"Undoubtedly. Did he say anything to you?"

"The guy in the supermarket? Of course not. I told you it was my imagination. The poor man probably lives in the neighborhood; that's why I recognized him."

157

"If he approaches you again, will you promise me you'll be careful?"

"If he approaches me at all, I promise I'll bash him with my purse and run like hell. Satisfied?"

"Temporarily." He intended to call Rankin the minute he finished his conversation with Laine.

"Jealous?"

"Insanely. I wish I were there right now to show you just how possessive I can be."

"Hmm, sounds good to me."

"You sound good to me. And you feel good and you taste good and . . . I'm going crazy. Change the subject."

"Okay, tell me about your house or apartment. What room are you in? What are you doing now?"

"Packing." The answer slipped out before he could stop himself. That much wasn't a lie, but he hoped to hell she'd let the comment drop. Eyeing the assortment of clothing strewn across his bed, his fingers involuntarily dug into the mattress supporting his muscled thighs. He was packing all right — for a trip to hell.

"Better throw in a raincoat. We've had a lot of rain lately."

"Thanks, I will." They were back to trivialities, mundane words meant to prolong the conversation. Drew knew he should tell her good-night and hang up, but he needed the sound of her voice, needed to feel close to her. Was just one more minute of tender torment too much to ask?

"Laine, will you do something for me?"

"Hmm."

"Take care of yourself. The world can get crazy sometimes. No midnight dashes to the convenience store or shopping alone, all right? Promise me?"

"Of course, but why?"

"Because I love you."

158

There was a long, very poignant silence.

"You . . . you've never said that before."

"I'm saying it now. I love you."

"Drew —"

"If anything hap—" He doubled his fist and brought it down hard on his thigh, then cleared his throat. "If anything, loving you has been the best part of my life."

"And being loved by you the best part of mine. Oh, Drew, I wish you were here beside me."

"So do I, love, so do I. I want you to sleep now and dream of me telling you how very much I want you and love you."

"And will you dream of me?"

"Always."

By mutual but unspoken consent, they hung up at the same time.

Then, with staccato jabs, Drew punched out another number.

"This is Kenyon," he said into the receiver. "Put Rankin on."

"Problem?" Rankin answered without preamble.

"Not if you're the man I think you are. Do you have a tail on Ms. Stewart?"

"Yes."

"Is he instructed to stay with her constantly?"

"Never out of his sight."

"Thanks." Drew felt as though a ton had been lifted from his shoulders.

"Don't thank me. She's a weak spot. It's called covering your butt."

"Sure. Just the same . . . thanks." Abruptly, Drew hung up the phone.

He sat staring at the phone for a few minutes longer. His hand reached forward again, then dropped to his knee, as if he had intended to make another call and then changed his mind.

It was no use. Calling her back would only be a mistake. No matter how badly he ached for her solace, he had no right to make the situation more difficult for her. It would be bad enough when she walked into the jury room the day after next, and discovered he wasn't there, wouldn't be there. Why cause her more distress by telling her she was under protective surveillance? No reasonable purpose could be served by calling her back. Nothing except hearing her say she loved him one more time. Nothing except he could tell her that regardless of what happened, he would always love her. Even if he never saw her again. Even if . . .

Enough! Negative thinking will get you killed and is detrimental to the whole operation. Beginning now, all thoughts are directed toward San Antonio — and Barlow.

Barlow. Forty-eight hours would see the end of a cat-and-mouse game that had continued for more years than Drew cared to count. Each time their paths crossed, the elusive Barlow somehow managed to slip from Drew's grasp like water through his fingers. But no more. This time, Rankin had formulated as foolproof a plan as any trap could possibly be.

Barlow would pay for all the drugs he'd peddled in Vietnam, all the weapons he'd stolen and sold to the highest bidder, all the lives he'd destroyed. Revenge would indeed be sweet. Methodically, Drew began to fold and pack his clothing, at the same time mentally reviewing all the information Rankin had given him.

They knew Barlow was to meet the two "buyers" at Los Angeles International sometime early the following afternoon. The three would then fly by private jet to San Antonio. Miller, the Reese employee turned informant, was to make contact with Barlow and his friends to finalize details of the purchase.

Drew and the others would be ready and waiting.

A deep frown furrowed Drew's brow. The risk level on an operation of this kind was very high. Everything must dovetail perfectly or the danger increased tenfold. Miller was the unknown factor and weakest link in the chain as far as Drew was concerned. In his experience, turncoats were an untrustworthy lot — he had little use for any of them. What methods had been used to convince Miller to work with the authorities, he didn't want to know. In far too many instances, the payoff for knowing details backfired.

The fact that the entire operation hinged on Miller made Drew apprehensive. Whenever possible, an agent was substituted in a similar situation, but Barlow knew Miller; if they pulled a ringer on Barlow at the last minute, he would never break cover.

Stuffing the last garment into his suitcase, Drew thought of how many times in his life he'd played this scene. Packing, checking, double-checking, going over plans in his head, thinking about the mission, blotting out all else. Mental fitness was every bit as important as physical fitness for such an operation. Allowing oneself to be sidetracked was suicidal. With mechanical movements he snapped the suitcase closed and for the millionth time, it seemed, placed the bag beside the door. Suddenly he felt much older than his years. Tired. And tired was a dangerous state of mind.

Abruptly, he snatched up a jacket and headed for the door. He had to shake the gloom threatening his equilibrium. Two steps outside, his shadow appeared.

"Kinda late to be goin' out, isn't it, Mr. Kenyon?"

"Can't sleep. Thought I'd go for a walk."

The shadow shook his head.

"Okay," Drew shrugged. "Then how 'bout I buy you a drink?"

161

"Mr. Kenyon." There was a note of warning in the shadow's voice as he took a step forward.

Drew cut him off with the wave of a hand. "I get the message. Don't need a hands-on translation."

"Good."

Drew gave the man a curt nod and returned to his room. He rammed both hands deep into his pants pockets and began to pace. Absently the fingers of his right hand sought, but did not find, his talisman.

He stopped dead still, remembering where he'd last seen his lucky charm, lying against soft, warm flesh. His life, her life; they were the same.

God in heaven, don't let me have come so close to happiness only to have it snatched away.

Dawn was glowing pink in the night sky before sleep finally granted him sweet release.

Chapter 11

"Ms. Stewart?"

Laine looked up from her perusal of the day's agenda into the grinning face of Miles Palmer, a highschool literature teacher and fellow juror. Palmer barely matched Laine's height and he sported a waistline that bespoke rich food and no exercise. His attempts to subdue an Alfalfa-like sprig of hair on the crown of his head always seemed to fail miserably. From her seated viewpoint, Laine thought he resembled a pear, complete with stem. She had always thought him pleasantly innocuous, but she sensed something different in his demeanor now. His normally sallow complexion was flushed with color.

"Yes."

"May I call you Laine?" His voice sounded hoarse and his pronounced Adam's apple bobbed rapidly up and down his throat.

"Certainly." Laine tilted her head to one side quizzically.

"I, uh, don't want to seem bold, but, I, uh, was wondering if you would consider having lunch with me today?" He glanced around nervously. The grand jury room was still almost empty.

"That's very nice of you, Mr. Palmer, but I already have plans today. Thank you anyway."

"What about tomorrow?"

Tomorrow she would see Drew. Going to lunch with Mild-mannered Miles was definitely not on Thursday's agenda. But his persistence was charming and she felt a little sorry for him. He was probably a very pleasant companion and obviously shy, or else why had he waited until the very last session to even approach her for a date?

"No, I'm sorry, but tomorrow is filled up."

"What about dinner this evening?"

"You're very sweet to ask, but I feel it only fair to tell you I'm not available at any time."

"You'd better reconsider." The color in his face darkened and he was no longer smiling. "I only want the same thing you offered to your prosecutor friend."

At the shocked expression on Laine's face, Palmer's smile returned. He shoved his hands into his pockets and rocked back and forth on his heels. "Thought that might change your mind." His smile became a self-satisfied smirk.

Laine stared at him in disbelief. Only a moment before, she had actually felt sorry for this oversize toad. "I don't know what you're talking about, Mr. Palmer. In any case, my answer stands." She turned back to the pages in front of her and tried to still the trembling in her hands.

How could he know anything? Had he observed the heated visual exchanges between her and Drew? Had he put two and two together and guessed that their attraction might extend past the casual? That had to be the answer — a good guess.

"Kissing in public parking lots is what I'm talking about. And quite a kiss it was, too, I must say."

Oh, Lord, he had seen them! Somehow Miles Palmer had witnessed that first, devastating kiss and now he intended to use what he saw against her. She would have to play the innocent.

"I'm sorry." Laine met his gaze steadfastly. "What did you say?" She pretended distraction compounded by disinterest.

"I said, 'You were kissing the prosecutor from Washington.' That wasn't very judicious of you, Laine. Good thing I was the one who saw you, and not one of the judges or even the district attorney."

Laine's trembling took on a different nature. She was shaking with anger. *The little toad is trying to blackmail me into going*

164

out with him! I'd like to wring his fat neck till his eyes bug out.

Unfortunately, she realized, retaliation was not the wisest course of action, for either her or Drew. No, she would have to bluff her way through and hope to hell she was a good-enough actress to pull it off.

She schooled her voice into an even, calm tone.

"Parking lot? Kissing? Me? I'm sorry to disappoint you, Mr. Palmer, but I'm afraid it wasn't me you saw. Do you spend a lot of time watching people in parking lots?" She wanted to throttle him.

"It was you. Look, I'm not asking for the moon — just a little TLC."

In her mind, TLC relative to Palmer translated to Total, Lecherous Cockroach!

She smiled as sweetly as she could with her teeth clenched.

"Mr. Palmer," she said in a soothing voice, "I'm flattered you see me in other women, but I really don't have the vaguest idea what you're talking about. Now, if you'll excuse me —"

"I wonder what the federal district attorney would think about my story?"

By now Laine's smile felt plastered to her face, but she intended to play her part right to the end. It was her only hope.

"I really couldn't say." Her offhanded response implied she could care less.

He eyed her suspiciously, then turned and stomped off in a huff.

Laine's stomach flip-flopped dangerously, her palms were dripping nervous perspiration and for a moment she thought she was going to be sick. *Oh, God, don't let that rotten little worm carry out his threat. Please, please.*

If Miles Palmer went to the federal district attorney with his suspicions, what would happen to Drew? Any hint of

165

scandal would probably damage his career. And what about the Reese case? Would his relationship with her prompt an investigation that might alter, or worse yet, even postpone the culmination of Drew's hard work? She needed to talk to Drew. He had to be told. She couldn't let him walk into the jury room unaware of the situation. But how could she reach him? He was probably on his way to the Washington airport by now.

It dawned on Laine, then, that Drew had been very vague about his plans. He hadn't even told her where he would be staying. Perhaps he felt the temptation to call him would have been too great. Perhaps. But in retrospect, she felt he had been deliberately evasive. Why? They both knew and accepted the fact that until her jury service ended on Friday, they were off-limits to each other.

The newest turn of events added confusion and more questions. How in the hell was she going to deal with Palmer? Changing her mind about going out with him now would be an admission of guilt and much too risky. Clearly the man was open to negotiation, but she didn't care for his rate of exchange. If Miles was gutsy enough to attempt blackmail, he was crazy enough to make good his threat. There was, she decided ruefully, nothing to do but stick by her original indignant reaction. She could blow it all on one roll of the dice, but she had no options left.

Grand jury members were filing into the room one by one, but their numbers were few. Laine counted heads. Fifteen, including herself. The panel was two short of a quorum. At that moment, Nelda Patterson popped through the open doorway and walked directly to Laine.

"We may have a real problem, dear."

"So I noticed."

"Three jurors have called in sick. Mr. Swanson's wife had

166

emergency gall-bladder surgery last night. That only leaves four possibles." She glanced at her watch. "Almost nine o'clock. Doesn't look good."

"What happens if we don't have a quorum?"

"We all go home and try again tomorrow. Or —" she shook her head in exasperation "— cancel the session completely and call another for next week. I'm not really sure what will be decided."

Cancellation! I won't be able to see Drew.

"Ah, here comes one of our lost sheep." The spritely secretary nodded to the juror who rushed into the room. "Sixteen down and one to go. Let's give it fifteen or twenty more minutes. If number seventeen doesn't show by then, I'll check with the D.A.'s office and see what they want to do. I can guarantee they will not be thrilled if we have to put everything on hold till next week. We're calling the no-shows right now. Maybe somebody overslept and is on their way in. Not to worry; be back in a wink." She gave Laine a reassuring smile, then marched from the jury room like a mother hen hell-bent on locating a missing chick. Laine stared after her, praying Nelda's mission would be successful.

"What's the story?" Donna Marshall sidled up beside Laine as soon as the secretary departed. "Looks like we're on the short side today."

Laine sighed and offered a half smile. "That about covers it."

"So, do we get the day off for good behavior, or what?"

"If juror seventeen doesn't show up soon, we may get the whole week off," Laine replied, a tinge of irritation creeping into her voice.

"Oh, goody." Donna rubbed her hands together gleefully. " 'Cause by then our little period of enlistment will be over."

"You haven't been mustered out yet," Laine warned. "If

we can't get it together today, we have to come back next week."

Donna Marshall uttered a very unladylike comment and then said, "Gimme a break! Eighteen months of doing my duty for God and country is the limit. To be honest, it's been fun at times, but enough's enough. My boss nearly has a coronary every time I have to take time off to come up here, anyway. He'll go off the deep end over two weeks in a row."

"Don't cry on my shoulder, we're all in the same boat." Laine's reply came out sharper than she intended. Her expression softened as she looked at Donna. "You're only saying what everyone else is thinking. We all expected this to be the last session and I think everyone is a little testy. Smile, maybe we'll get luc—"

"Number seventeen!" Donna squealed, pointing at a flustered Ruth Jackson, who scurried into the jury room followed by a smiling Nelda Patterson.

"Troops present and accounted for," Nelda said to Laine and Donna. "Charge!" She gave the two women a cockeyed salute and departed.

The morning session was slow and suffered several interruptions. No testimony could be heard unless all seventeen jurors were present. And because the quorum had barely been established, whenever a juror needed to leave the room, the entire presentation came to a halt. The reduced assembly made voting difficult as hell. A majority vote of twelve of the seventeen was required for an indictment on any case. Two presentations involving mail fraud and one regarding possession of dangerous drugs culminated in a vote and lengthy, arduous discussion among the jurors. Several times, debate among the panel members became rather heated. Painstakingly aware of her leadership role, Laine found herself in the position of devil's advocate more than once.

On the drug case her vote provided the majority. Even though in her own mind she was sufficiently convinced of the man's guilt to vote for indictment, she felt an uneasiness over the fact that her "yes" had decided the plaintiff would go to trial and very possibly to prison.

Athough small in number, the group was no less conscientious. All questions had to be answered to every juror's satisfaction. People's lives, careers and reputations hung in the balance. The jurors had to be certain — beyond a shadow of a doubt — that enough evidence was present to proceed with an indictment.

By noon, tension was evident in all the jurors' faces. Laine prayed the afternoon session would be less taxing. Several case discussions had become heated, plus she could swear that Miles Palmer was leering at her every time she glanced in his direction. Her concentration was sporadic at best.

Her mind continually strayed to Drew. One minute she wondered if he would call her, wondered if by some miracle they could be together; the next, she berated herself for even entertaining such dangerous thoughts. He had to be told of Palmer's blackmail threat; but how and when?

Absorbed in her anxieties, Laine gazed out the window of the federal courthouse, unmindful of the sunlight glistening on glass buildings, indeed of anything but her own musings. A tap on her shoulder brought her thoughts abruptly back into focus.

"Ms. Stewart?"

Laine whipped her head around, startled.

"Sorry," Nelda Patterson apologized with a smile. "Another change. Bless your heart, y'all have just had more than you can say grace over today, haven't you?" She handed Laine an addendum to the case schedule.

"Is this the rest of today's schedule?"

"Yes," Nelda said distractedly while searching through the cumbersome files in her hand. "Oh, Good Lord!" She yanked a piece of paper from the stack. "That's not today's agenda, it's Thursday's. Child, I don't know what's got into me." She exchanged pages with Laine. "It's all these changes. That prosecutor from Washington is back and I think they're going to want a vote today."

Laine's heart skipped several beats.

Drew. Drew was here!

"Th . . . thank you," she managed to stammer as the secretary disappeared from view. Her cold fingers gripped the paper so tightly the edges curled under the pressure.

In a few minutes Drew would walk through the door and her world would be right again.

She wanted to squeal with joy, jump, shout. She wanted to race to the door, throw her arms around his neck and smother him with kisses. None of that was possible, but just knowing she would be in the same room with him was enough to make her lightheaded and deliriously happy. Palmer's threat — indeed, all else — was relegated to the far corners of her mind. Dizzy with elation and anticipation, she fixed her gaze on the door to the jury room.

He would smile at her and she could smile back. They would be together. In every aspect, save physically, they would be one. She closed her eyes and allowed herself a brief but sustained memory of his touch, his voice.

"Good afternoon, ladies and gentlemen. It's a pleasure to see you again."

Laine's eyes flew open. A tiny gasp of shock slipped from her lips and she blinked. The familiar voice did not belong to Drew Kenyon.

Warren Elroy stood at the prosecutor's table.

Laine glanced at the closed door of the jury room. Drew

was late. Perhaps his flight had been delayed. Or perhaps he was in the office collecting last-minute information. But he would be here. He'd told her he would be in Texas by . . .

"Once again, I find myself substituting for Mr. Kenyon, but I've become quite taken with your city so you'll hear no complaints from me." Elroy smiled broadly at the jurors.

Laine had a complaint, but no place to register it.

Where was Drew?

"Our testimony during the last session dealt mainly with giving the members of the grand jury sufficient background, along with investigatory findings, in order to proceed with indictment. Timing, I might add, has been an essential factor in this case. We've received word that the target of this investigation is making his move, so it's time for us to go into action."

As he spoke, Elroy crossed the room and handed Laine the legal-sized sheets of paper containing the typed indictment. She stared at the document as if it were some loathsome and totally foreign object.

"With your permission, Madam Foreman, I will read the indictment, then give a summary of previous testimony." In a smooth, precise voice Warren Elroy defined the prosecution's charges against the man called Barlow. Details of the CIA agent's testimony were highlighted as well as the government's nefarious plans to capture the infamous Mr. Barlow. Not only did Uncle Sam hope to snare a traitor, but to secure the millions offered for Barlow's merchandise into the bargain.

Treason, espionage, possession of stolen firearms, violation of the Interstate Commerce Act, nine counts in all, each requiring a separate vote.

Mr. Elroy finished reading and turned to Laine. "Does the grand jury have any questions?"

There was silence for a second, then one of the older ladies

171

at the far table raised her hand.

"I know we're not supposed to consider this man Barlow's past criminal record, but didn't Mr. Kenyon tell us he was a known traitor?"

"Known and proven are two different things," Elroy pointed out. "But to answer your question — yes, Donald Barlow does have a long history of subversive activity."

"And the tapes we asked you to verify?" came a question from Laine's right.

"The tapes introduced into evidence, which you heard at the last session, have been examined thoroughly by the FBI and the CIA. There's no question the man speaking was Donald Barlow."

"And the guy in San Antonio — he contacted Barlow, not the other way around?"

"Yes. But regardless of how contact was made, the tapes prove Barlow has connections all over the world and is ready and willing to negotiate the sale of the weapons to a foreign power. Barlow, not the Reese employee, suggested the purchase and distribution route so that the guns might eventually wind up in Libya. Barlow established the amount of the sale and how it was to be handled. And Barlow has commanded the operation since the first time he was approached. I stress to each of you, all the evidence supports the fact that Donald Barlow travels with the insurrectionary elements in our society. He is an admitted mercenary with no loyalties to any government or political ideologies, save his own greed. With your help we hope to get him, the unnamed foreign agents and the money, all at one time. Yes?" Elroy pointed to the dentist who had his hand up.

"What is the penalty for treason?"

"It depends." Elroy frowned. "Life imprisonment. Death penalty in some cases."

172

Laine tapped her pencil loudly on the table. "Please remember," she cautioned, "our job here is to indict based on the evidence presented. We are deciding whether or not this man should be brought to a court of law. If we start considering possible sentencing before we begin to deliberate, I think we would be defeating the purpose of the grand jury. I know it's hard not to think about what will happen if he's found guilty, but try not to."

"Thank you, Ms. Stewart."

Laine's admonition to the jurors was as much for herself as for them. The uneasiness of the morning's voting battle had returned full-blown.

She cut a sideways glance at Miles Palmer. And what if they questioned her vote after the story Palmer intended to tell the district attorney? Would the authorities say Drew had somehow influenced her vote? But if she voted "no," would there be enough "yes" votes to indict? There was allowance for only five dissenting votes. Or possibly four and an abstention.

Yes. If she didn't vote at all, the question of Drew's influence was moot.

"Are there any more questions?" Elroy waited patiently, receiving no response. "Then I shall leave you to your duty." He left the room.

"Are we ready to call the vote?" Laine's nervous fingers almost dropped the document as she handed the sheaf of papers to Donna Marshall to record and tally the vote. Laine rose and pushed the chair away from her slightly. She straightened the collar of her dress then spoke in a firm tone of voice.

"Count one. How many vote against indictment?"

Four jurors raised their hands.

Laine's heart raced. She was almost home free.

"How many vote for indictment?

Eleven hands shot into the air.

A tiny shudder ripped through Laine. The count wasn't enough. Someone other than herself had not voted. Unless the vote changed, the grand jury would have to hand down a "No Bill" and Barlow and his coconspirators would go free. All Drew's hard work would be for naught.

"This is ridiculous!" A man at the far table jumped to his feet. "I can't believe we're gonna do this. We're gonna let him go. Which two of you didn't vote?" The question was riddled with criticism.

"Well, I . . . ." All eyes turned to the young housewife. "I wasn't sure, so I figured it was better not to vote at all than vote the wrong way."

"What in tarnation are you not sure about?" Ruth asked in a disgusted tone of voice. "Short of a signed confession, I don't know what more you could want. It's right there in black and white. The man is going to sell weapons to a procommunist country. Weapons that could wind up killing American boys. My Lord!"

"Now, wait a minute. The girl has a right to her opinions," someone inserted.

"But she doesn't *have* an opinion," another juror countered.

"Then she's not been listening," came a still-further comment.

"Please!" Laine commanded in a firm voice. She looked at the young woman under harassment. "Exactly what is preventing you from making a decision one way or the other?"

Laine prayed the same question wouldn't be asked of her.

"Well, treason is a pretty big deal."

"You're damned right it is!" The male juror who had jumped to his feet earlier maintained his fighting stance.

"Please," Laine ordered, though this time her tone of voice was less harsh.

"I mean, you see spies on TV and the movies, but . . . ."

174

The young woman shrugged helplessly. "I just never thought I'd be faced with putting one in jail."

"But you're not," Ruth interrupted, before Laine could respond. "Even if we indict him, he has to be caught and tried before he could go to prison. He'll have his day in court. If he's innocent, the other jury will know it. If he's not guilty, they won't send the man to jail just because we said there was just cause to try him. Now tell me the truth," Ruth demanded like an irate mother talking to a misbehaving child. "Deep down in your heart, do you really have even a tiny doubt about voting 'yes' on this indictment?"

The young housewife vacillated for a second before answering, "No, not really. I guess I was just kind of scared by the idea of all that responsibility. Can I change my vote?"

Laine nodded brusquely. "Let's start from the top. All those in favor of voting 'yes' for count one, raise your hands?"

Fourteen.

It seemed that two other votes had changed. There was a smattering of applause from the agreeing jurors.

"Count one, against?"

Two.

"Count two." Laine rushed to announce the next count to forestall any questions about the total.

And so it went, until the ninth count had been recorded. Laine's sigh of relief was cut short by the sound of Miles Palmer's voice.

"Didn't we have one person abstain?" Palmer glanced around the room, carefully avoiding eye contact with the foreman.

"I did." Laine's voice was calm, cool. She knew that trying to evade the question would only bring more questions.

"How come?" someone asked.

Laine pretended concentration as she signed her name to

the line at the bottom of each indictment. "My reasons were personal."

"Did you ever stop to think your so-called personal reasons might have set loose a traitor?" Palmer had no intention of letting her off the hook.

"My conscience is completely clear on that score, Mr. Palmer. I will always be in favor of justice for anyone who attempts to manipulate and abuse people for his own selfish gain. I would have voted to break a tie." Laine's eyes sparked amber bolts of electricity as she pierced her opponent with her gaze.

They fought a war of visual slings and arrows, defiance against intimidation. Finally, Palmer wilted under the heat of Laine's gaze and backed off with a disgruntled "Humph."

"Let's take a break." The jurors greeted Laine's suggestion with open gratitude.

Laine didn't join the others, but stayed behind trying to sort out the events of the afternoon. She replayed her telephone conversation with Drew over and over in her head. Had he lied to her? If not, what had happened at the last moment to deter him from coming to Dallas? If he were no longer connected with the Reese case, most of their worries would be over. But wouldn't he have known there might be such a possibility? And if that were true, surely Drew would have mentioned it. Wouldn't he?

Of course he would. You're making mountains out of molehills. Don't let your imagination run wild.

But between telling and convincing there is a wide gulf to be bridged and Laine was unable to persuade herself not to worry about the puzzling turn of events. She had to talk to Drew, but didn't have the vaguest idea how to reach him. Who would know, and how could she inquire without causing suspicion?

The logical person was Warren Elroy. Damn! Why hadn't

she asked about Prosecutor Kenyon while Elroy was still in the room? If she sought him out now, he might think her query more than a little unusual. Maybe Nelda Patterson could help her, Laine reasoned. If she were very careful about her approach to the subject, surely the secretary would know the comings and goings of the prosecutors. *Someone* in Washington must have given a reason for the substitution. Even the government can't say "Do this and do that" without an explanation.

Can't they? a tiny voice asked. What justification was given when they snatched Drew from Cancún? None. And what rationale had Drew given when he had told her there was no one else to take over the Reese case? None. But someone else had taken Drew's place and now no reason was given for the switch.

Her head throbbed. A slightly shaky hand rubbed her furrowed brow. No rhyme or reason. Nothing made sense. Nothing except her love for Drew and even that was beginning to sound senseless in view of his second "disappearance."

She *must* have some answers. And if she had to lie through her teeth to get them, so be it. Nelda Patterson had no way of knowing she was about to be confronted by a desperate woman, and desperate women can be very cunning and extremely tenacious.

Watching the jurors straggle slowly back into the jury room, Laine sensed their reluctance to face another round of voting. However, the worst was over. Only the few presentations from the morning session required votes. Once accomplished, the panel waited to be summoned by the judge, whereupon the indictments were presented and verified. The panel would then be dismissed until the next day.

Laine, however, had no intention of going home without some answers. Carefully she plotted to corner Nelda with a trumped-up but pertinent question.

As soon as the remaining indictments were voted upon, Laine quickly gathered all the documents in her arms, telling Donna she had decided to walk the papers to Nelda's office herself.

"Oh, aren't you sweet. But you didn't have to bring those yourself. I was just about to fetch them." The secretary smiled as Laine sailed through the office door and deposited the stack of signed indictments on the desk.

"No problem." Laine returned the smile. "We are through except for seeing the judge, aren't we?"

"Absolutely. We ran y'all ragged today and Judge Thompson will probably be available within the hour, so with any luck y'all will be out of here in time to beat the rush-hour traffic."

"Great. I, uh, was wondering if you could tell me anything about tomorrow's agenda. It's the last day, you know, and several of the jurors asked about bringing in some food. Nothing fancy — sort of a farewell luncheon."

"How lovely!" Nelda clasped her hands in front of her chest in a uniquely old-fashioned gesture. "The schedule won't be nearly as crowded; in fact . . ." Her voice trailed off as she shuffled through a pile of folders. "There are only three presentations, all fairly short. I believe you could safely assume y'all will be footloose and fancy-free by noon."

"Fine. Oh, by the way, some of the jurors were curious about why the government changed prosecutors in midstream, so to speak, on the treason case. Mr. Kenyon's name was still listed as attorney on my printed agenda, yet Mr. Elroy showed up."

"And I'll just bet the jurors who asked were ladies, right?" Nelda Patterson grinned.

"Right." Laine laughed.

"Hmm, that Kenyon fella made a couple of hearts in our

office turn over, too. Sorry about the error on the agenda. It should have listed Elroy as presenter. Mr. Kenyon's name was removed as attorney of record shortly after the last session."

"Oh, I — we thought Mr. Elroy was a substitute brought in at the last minute."

"Heavens no, dear. Mr. Elroy has been handling everything since last month. We never expected anyone but him."

"I see." Frantically, Laine racked her brain trying to find another way to gain more information without being obvious. "No big deal." She shrugged her shoulders nonchalantly. "I must admit, though, the case is probably the most intriguing one we've heard. CIA, FBI, foreign spies. All of us are simply dying to know the outcome. Do you think they will tell us?"

"Well, I do know Mr. Elroy is not scheduled to return to Washington until tomorrow afternoon. Perhaps he can be persuaded to drop by in the morning and give you the straight scoop." There was a decided sparkle in Nelda Patterson's bright eyes. "From the scuttlebutt I've heard, by tomorrow it should all be over but the shouting, anyway." She arched an eyebrow at Laine in a manner that might be construed as conspiratorial.

"What do you mean by 'it' will all be over?"

"Just speculation, but if two and two still equals four . . . ? Well, think about it. Why would they be in a hurry to call for indictments today unless they were ready to move. This office has instructions to issue arrest warrants as soon as the judge approves the indictments. When these guys decide to move, they move!"

"I see what you mean." Laine tried to make her response sound blasé, when she was anything but. She wanted to reach across the desk and demand, physically if necessary, the rest of the information from the secretary. But she couldn't. She had a feeling that Nelda had already said more than was prudent.

"Well, let's get these to Judge Thompson so y'all can go home."

"Yes, it has been a long day."

An even longer night followed for Laine inside her apartment. The walls seemed to close in around her. With only her anguished thoughts for company, she felt caged within her own home.

A pot of coffee perked while she changed into a comfortable velour robe. Barely tasting the rich, dark brew, she sipped her first cup and began a retracing of the day's events, which would take her way into the night.

Every word Drew had said to her since their first meeting was replayed, the dialogue rearranged inside her head like pieces of a jigsaw puzzle. The solution was there; she simply couldn't see it. Yet, convinced that somewhere, in something he'd said, lay the answers, Laine began a mental search-and-rescue mission as she paced across the soft beige carpet of her living room.

He'd withdrawn from the Reese case, then returned without hesitation, giving the impression he could take no other course of action. Why? Because some sort of pressure had been applied? Or because of his own personal integrity?

He'd vanished from her life and reappeared with very little explanation. Had he cared so little that he didn't feel the need to explain? Or was it, perhaps, that he couldn't have done so without breaking some rule?

Drew had made the kind of love and promises only a stupid man would contemplate if he were lying. If she were just another in a long line of conquests, she reasoned logically, why not let the affair die a natural death? Why keep up the pretense?

Laine's bare feet shuffled over the thick carpet until her soles grew warm. Tired, frustrated and sick with worry, she shoved her knotted fists into the pockets of her robe and headed for her fourth refill of coffee.

Inside one pocket, her knuckles came into contact with a small cylindrical metal object. She stopped dead in her tracks. Her heartbeat jumped to an erratic drumming and goose bumps scampered up her arms. Drew's good-luck piece! During their phone conversation the evening before, she had fondled the charm lovingly while the sound of his voice soothed her soul.

Trembling fingers closed around the object that seemed to move into her palm as though it were alive.

Slowly, she withdrew her hand and opened her fist to reveal the good-luck charm. She stared at the bullet for long moments, seeing instead the image of Drew's beloved face. The memory of their last night together washed over her, flooding her with all the colors of love. Softly whispered words came back to haunt her.

I trust you with my life.

He had kissed her then, his wide hand covering her breast and the good-luck charm, his lips and tongue imprinting her body as his gift had imprinted her soul — indelibly, endlessly, forever.

The talisman came into focus through a bittersweet rain of tears as Laine returned from the mist of the memory. Cheeks wet with tears, she clutched the good-luck piece tightly to her chest. An aching greater than any she'd known filled her heart and mind.

"My love," she whispered to the empty room. "I know only you are my love and I am yours. Wherever you are, whatever the circumstances, God keep you safe and bring you back to me."

Chapter 12

Drew wiped perspiration from his face onto the sleeve of his black T-shirt, already damp from repeated use. The cricket chorus, loud in the night air, accompanied the rhythmic thud of his own heartbeat. His body shifted, seeking a less uncomfortable position. God, how he hated all the waiting, the watching, the sweating — the endless minutes of inaction. He checked the time: 10:45. An hour and fifteen minutes more to go.

With the steamy dampness of warm earth beneath him and a starless Texas sky above, Drew lay stretched full-length on the grassy knoll. Tiny rocks, half buried in the soil, felt like melon-size boulders as their jagged edges dug through his heavy cotton pants and into his legs. No such protrusions, however, irritated his flesh from collarbone to groin. Not even a rock with a razor-sharp edge could be felt through the lightweight but impenetrable body armor pressed against his torso. Beneath a black watch cap his blond hair was plastered to his head. Sweat trickled down his face, causing the night-vision goggles to slip downward occasionally over the bridge of his nose.

Drew adjusted the focus as he scanned the area. The goggles, using ambient light, gave the effect of viewing the world through a highly magnified computer screen. His field of vision was a phosphorescent green made mobile by the constantly moving restricted light, the infrared LED lenses giving the abandoned airstrip an eerie, ghostlike quality.

Drew shifted his weight again, elbows planted firmly into a section of flattened grass, as his lean fingers fine-tuned the focus of the night glasses. Slowly his gaze swept the terrain in an arc from the far side of the deserted runway, around the end of the concrete slab and across the knee-high grass as he checked the locations of his companions. Similarly dressed, geared and lying flat against the earth, they, too, waited and watched.

Tiny battery-operated "fireflies" clipped to each agent's belt pinpointed the members of the team with their flashes. Indiscernible to the naked eye but visible through the night-vision glasses, the five blinking lights formed a north-to-south semicircle approximately one hundred feet from the edges of the runway. The minibeacons identified the good guys from the bad guys. Like numbers on the face of a clock, with the landing strip running through the center, the men were stationed at eleven, one, three, five and six. Drew's position, between seven and eight, gave him a clear sweep of the entire team and the rendezvous spot.

Lens to lens, Drew exchanged "okay" hand signals with each man, the visual reconnaissance ending with the agent stationed across one of the many gullies that snaked through the land about fifty feet to Drew's right. Less than a mile away, CIA and local law-enforcement officers were preparing highly sophisticated listening and recording equipment — equipment that would insure Barlow's conviction once he was arrested.

Like a deserted stage, the abandoned slab of concrete cut across the terrain west to east, awaiting the arrival of the last in tonight's cast of players. Darkness prevailed, yet there was no sign of Miller. For what seemed like the hundredth time in the past hour, Drew mentally reviewed the voice tape of the late-afternoon meeting between Miller and Barlow.

"How . . . how was your flight?" Miller's feeble attempt to be polite was betrayed by the nervousness so evident in his voice.

"Don't strain yourself, Miller. This is not a social call."

Silence, followed by the sound of chairs scraping against

the barroom floor and the rustling of clothes.

"Did you make all the arrangements?" Barlow's gravelly-voiced questioning was terse. Miller must have nodded. "Exactly as I instructed?"

"Exactly."

The sound of paper crinkled, then Barlow's reply was almost mumbled. "Good."

"Can we get this over with, Barlow? Why in the hell did you insist on a face-to-face meeting anyway?"

"I like to look a man in the eye when I do business with him. Sort of the personal touch, you might say." Drew remembered the feral smile in Barlow's recorded voice.

"All right, but let's make it pronto."

"Fine. Where?"

"Ah, there's several old auxiliary airstrips in the area. The military once used them for flight training, but most have been abandoned since Vietnam, 'cept the ones over by Rand—"

"You're babbling like an idiot, Miller. Which one?"

"Out toward Marion, 'bout twenty miles northeast of Randolph Air Force Base. It hasn't been used in over eight years for anything but locals flying their model airplanes on Sunday."

"Suitable. What time?"

"Midnight."

"Agreed. My traveling companions will join us."

"Now just a damn minute, Barlow. You wanna make this deal person to person between us, fine. But I'm not about to have a couple of your ex-camel merchants turned oil barons thrown in for good measure. Those hawk-nosed dudes make me nervous."

A sharp crunching noise preceded Barlow's reply. "Everything makes you nervous, Miller. My friends are very cautious buyers. They want to make sure they're getting their money's worth. So it's either four for tonight, or no deal."

There was a long silence, at the end of which Miller must have nodded.

"Good. They also want to see a sample before they buy."

"What! Have you lost your mind? You saw the . . . the . . . merchandise. Isn't your word good enough for 'em?" Miller's query rose an octave and a couple of decibels.

"Shut up!" Barlow's grainy-voiced command hissed over the tape. "You're attracting attention. Stop making an ass out of yourself and listen." Another silence. "Have the entire shipment ready to transfer just as we planned, only keep it out of sight till my friends satisfy themselves of the quality. Then we can complete the deal right on the spot. Don't get your tail feathers ruffled. These guys are a strange breed; they do everything very carefully. Don't sweat it. I know what I'm doing."

"Yeah, but do you know what they're doing?"

"Every minute."

Silence again, then Miller cleared his throat.

"The, uh, transaction is, uh, strictly C.O.D., you know."

"You deliver what you've promised and you'll get paid. I trust your man on the inside can meet our demand?"

"Yeah." Silence.

"Say, uh, if everything goes right, you think maybe these guys might be interested in buying more stuff?"

A chair creaked as though someone had slowly leaned forward.

"Miller, I'm only going to say this once: After tonight, I don't ever want to see or hear from you again, unless I notify you. Like my companions, I am a very cautious man. Repeated transactions with the same individual are too easy to trace. Don't get greedy, Miller; you'll live longer."

"Sh— sure, sure. I was only —"

"You were only nothing. Remember, I want you there at eleven to check the place out one more time. If anything looks

185

fishy to you, put out a flare like you've had car trouble. If I don't see the flare, I'll be there at midnight."

The creaking sound came again, followed by a scraping noise, and conversation ceased. A long silence, then Miller's voice delivered a very descriptive, profane assessment of Barlow's character and ancestry.

Drew's mental tape recorder clicked off and his jaw tightened. Barlow's scratchy, faint Boston accent still grated on his nerves as badly as ever; but then, everything about Barlow went against Drew's grain. The man was a viper, the lowest form of reptilian vermin, representing everything Drew was against. Barlow slithered and crawled through the world, causing everything he touched to rot and die. There were very few men whom Drew Kenyon actually hated — but he hated Donald Barlow. From the jungles of Vietnam to the Texas hill country, their conflict spanned more than miles and years for the two adversaries; it also spanned opposing morals, life-styles and values.

Drugs, prostitution, secret documents, weapons — you name it; Barlow would sell anything to anybody for the right price. Unfortunately, human life was a cheap commodity. Drew knew Barlow held little regard for any life other than his own and he would never submit to arrest. He also knew that Barlow was a crack shot.

Drew checked his watch and frowned. Ten fifty-eight and still Miller was a no-show. The SOB was sure cutting it close. Perhaps the guys in the equipment van had been a little slow with the wiring job on Miller. Everything had to be perfect; they couldn't risk months of hard work being ruined because of a loose connection or a faulty battery. Sweat rolled down the side of his face and dripped from his chin. God, but he hated the waiting. *Counting minutes can be a dangerous pastime. Come on, Kenyon, checklist time.*

186

Pushing the night goggles to his forehead, his thumb and index finger rubbed the bridge of his nose as Drew methodically began his mental review. Goggles, 9 mm automatic pistol, knife, body bug — he reached to check the transmitter at his waist and the flexible antenna that ran halfway up his back — and last, his assault rifle.

Next came the sequence of preplanned events. Miller should arrive any second. Barlow and friends would arrive at midnight. Allow fifteen minutes for show and tell. As far as the buyers knew, they would take the merchandise, pay the tab, then everyone would return to his respective vehicle and drive off into the night. But Drew and his companions were about to rewrite the scenario, giving the ending an unexpected twist. As soon as the money was in Miller's hands, he would give the signal and the company of agents would terminate Barlow's infamous career.

Unaccountably, an uneasiness settled over Drew. Every segment of the operation had to dovetail precisely, and he had the feeling that something didn't fit. He could sense it, but before he could name his niggling apprehension a single set of headlights precipitately dotted the night. Twin beams moved toward Drew's position until they were glaring spots of white; then they went black. He quickly lowered the goggles into place and once again the surrounding countryside turned ghostly green.

Less than twenty feet from the end of the runway, Miller's road-weary Bronco braked to a stop, the engine ceased, then a door slammed. Through his headset, Drew heard gravel crunching beneath booted feet as Miller walked around the truck, leaned against the door facing Drew, then began to fumble in his shirt pocket. The sound of a striking match rasped in Drew's ears as he watched Miller light a cigarette, then flip the burnt matchstick into the weeds. The man's movements

187

were jerky. His head turned slowly as if scanning the tall grass, seeking to verify the agents' presence. The glowing tip of the cigarette arced downward and fingers tapped the microphone hidden behind his oversize belt buckle. Drew was quick to notice Miller's hands were shaking as he yanked a handkerchief from a back pocket and wiped his face.

"Damn," Drew whispered, "he's going to blow the whole thing if he's not careful. What the hell is he doing? He knows the schedule." Miller's obvious nervousness augmented Drew's disquiet and he could not seem to shake the feeling that something was definitely wrong. In fact, as he peered into the darkness, the sensation grew stronger by the minute.

Again the night was disturbed as twin dots of light appeared at the far end of the runway.

The sound of gravel spitting from beneath tires broke the stillness. Simultaneously, Miller shot away from the truck and spun into place. The hair on the back of Drew's neck stood erect. His head snapped around. An unimpressive sedan rolled out of the darkness and into his field of vision.

The car stopped approximately thirty feet behind the truck and three men got out and walked toward Miller. Two of the passengers Drew had never seen, the third he would never forget.

Barlow!

Dammit to hell, the son of a bitch has deliberately jumped the gun! Drew's hard fist hit the ground beside his face with a muted thump. *So, that's why Miller acted so nervous when he got out of the truck — he was trying to let us know Barlow had changed the time.* Did Barlow suspect anything, or was he being his usual cautious self? *Those guys in the van better be on their toes or this whole thing could go down the dumper, quick!* Every muscle and nerve in Drew's body stretched taut as piano wire. It was too late to do anything except play out the assigned parts.

The cast was assembled.

The four men came together between the two vehicles. Miller, a full head taller than the others, seemed to shrink as Barlow approached.

"Do you have all of them?" Barlow said without preamble. At the other man's nod he announced, "Let's see the goods."

"Are these your buyers?"

"Let's just say these gentlemen are representing the buyers. They're here to insure nothing goes wrong."

Miller eyed the two Arabs nervously. They were so brawny their suits looked as if they were a size too small.

"At your service." Miller's voice and smile were strained as he popped open the tailgate of the fourwheel-drive truck and climbed inside. He squatted, balanced on the balls of his feet and jerked the corner of a tarpaulin aside, then withdrew a shoe-box-size container. Duck-walking clumsily in the back of the Bronco, he offered the container to Barlow.

"Show my friends your little toy and what it can do."

Miller turned, placed the box on the extended metal ledge, flipped the top open and extracted the contents . . . first the power pack, which he quickly clipped to his belt, then the pistol.

Click. Miller released the safety, lifted the gun and pretended to take aim, then lowered the weapon and handed it to the nearest foreigner. The power pack remained clipped to Miller's belt. The dark-complexioned man moved closer as Miller spoke.

"With this little jewel, one man has the firepower of twenty. It's a ruby laser with a maximum range of three hundred yards. Whatever it hits vaporizes. It can slice a man in half, clean as a whistle, or sizzle a selected square inch of his flesh to cinders. Really somethin', huh?" Impatiently, Miller shifted his weight from foot to foot while his gaze darted from one foreigner to the other.

Restricted by the almost-invisible cord connecting the power to the weapon, the man holding the gun turned and conversed with his countryman in rapid Arabic for several minutes before he handed the weapon back to Miller. They gestured for Miller to demonstrate the gun.

"Jesus, Barlow, are they crazy? I can't just start shootin' this thing. Why the hell can't they take anybody's word for anything?"

"Quit bitchin' and do it," Barlow instructed hoarsely.

"Like hell! I might as well take out a newspaper ad —"

In a split second Barlow wedged himself between Miller and the intended buyer and snatched the weapon from the taller man's grasp before he could prevent It. With the speed of a striking snake, he fired, slicing the darkness with a straight beam of ruby laser light. The blazing streak hit a knoll about fifty yards away.

Instinctively, Drew flattened his body against the ground as a spot of earth erupted a foot away, spraying him with clods of dirt. Mind and body poised on the rigid edge of alertness, his clothes sodden with sweat, adrenaline rocketed through Drew's veins. The strongest instinct known to man demanded he respond in kind and he fought the impulse to end Barlow's treacherous existence then and there.

Easy. Easy. Hang on. He forced his erratic breathing back to a more even rhythm.

"You crazy bastard!" Miller made a move toward Barlow only to find himself restrained by the hamfisted foreigners. Barlow faced the threesome, the barrel of the pistol pointed directly at Miller's chest.

"I thought you were stupid the first time I met you, Miller, and the last few minutes confirm my opinion. Our business is at an end. I find I no longer require your services." Barlow looked at one of the men holding Miller. "Take him into the field."

190

"No! Wait!" Miller yelped.

Now! Drew thought. They should move now! Miller was too panicked to remember the signal. *Where the hell are the others? We can't wait much longer.* Night glasses in place, he jerked his head slightly to the right and exchanged predetermined at-the-ready hand signals with the agent in command on the far side of the runway.

"Wait? For what, Miller? For you to beg?"

"I . . . I . . . people know where I am. There will be questions. Don't . . . don't. If it's the money, let's talk. I'll negotiate."

"You have nothing to negotiate, Miller. You're just a means to an end as far as I'm concerned; and you turn my stomach." Barlow raised the gun.

"No-o-o!" Miller screamed. "It's a trap! Don't shoot, don't shoot! FBI! Cops! Everywhere!"

Move! came the signal.

Drew yanked the goggles from his head, slammed them to the ground, shot into a crouching stance and brought his rifle to position in one smooth motion. Without hesitation he aimed and fired at the gun in Barlow's hand.

All hell broke loose.

Through the infrared sight, Drew saw the laser pistol cannonball from Barlow's hand, its force ripping the cord from the power pack still attached to Miller's belt. Miller's body jerked as if controlled by a master puppeteer. The Arabs released him like a hot poker and bolted for the car, drawing their own weapons as they went. A bullet whizzed over the top of the car as an agent moved to block the Arabs' escape. Two more shots rang out and the air in the rear tires of the sedan hissed into the darkness. The second agent fired a shot over the truck.

Another gun miraculously appeared from inside Barlow's

jacket and he wheeled toward Miller, who was now racing for the open area between the first and second agents. Barlow's bullet caught Miller squarely in the back of the head. He fell face-down, spread-eagled on the unyielding runway. Drew and the other agents were moving in, crawling through the tall grass toward their objective.

Barlow gripped his gun and made a desperate lunge through the yawning back end of the Bronco. Belly down, heaving with the effort to breathe, his mind screamed out in rage: *Kenyon, you bastard — You're out there somewhere and I'm going to get you!* With that thought he began to crawl forward, the sound of sporadic gunfire still coming from the sedan.

"FBI! It's over, Barlow. Give it up!" A voice from the grass boomed the order as in the distance the sound of approaching vehicles roared in the night.

"You in the car! Throw down your weapons!" Another round of shots replied.

The over-anxious agent to Drew's right raised his body a fraction too high. A bullet caught him in the chest, spun him around at just the right angle for another bullet to strike the upper middle of his back with the force of death.

A fresh tidal wave of rage rushed over Drew as he watched his comrade fall. Desire for revenge seized Drew in its unrelenting grip. Barlow *had* to die.

With a single-minded vengeance, Drew crawled toward the truck.

Barlow's hand was steady as, lying between the bucket seats of the Bronco, he reached up and grasped the key in the ignition. With a deft economy of motion, he brought the engine whirring to life; then, with his other hand, pressed the accelerator flat against the floor.

Drew jerked to his knees the instant the truck began to move. "Stop him!" In response, an agent directly in front of the Bronco took aim at the front windshield and fired.

Simultaneously, as the truck shot over the end of the runway and out across the dark terrain, a white van careened into the besieged area. Men poured from its flung-open doors, their weapons drawn. Another round of gunfire erupted from the sedan; the shots went wild.

Searing, white-hot pain exploded across the left side of Drew's head.

He swayed. The ground came dangerously near as he fought to retain consciousness. The pain inside his head was rioting to rip free and consume him. Vision blurry, he turned toward the truck in time to catch a horrifying glimpse of an agent a split second before the Bronco smashed into him, tossing his body aside like so much unwanted rubbish. Through vision distorted with agony and fury, Drew watched in sickening frustration as the truck zigzagged across the landscape, roaring wildly toward escape.

All gunfire from the sedan ceased. Reinforcements swarmed around Drew and the remaining agents who raced after the vehicle. Suddenly, the right front of the Bronco pitched forward, striking a mound of dirt. With a violent jarring, the vehicle thrashed from side to side, then reared into the air; its back wheels hit the mound with a guttural grinding sound. Hanging suspended in the air for a second, it plunged to earth, nosediving into a wide gully. Both doors snapped open and the gaping tailgate protruded skyward, resembling a panting tongue, as the rear wheels spun furiously.

A deadly darkness rapidly ate away at Drew's consciousness, dimmed his vision, crowded out the shouts of his compatriots, dulled the warm, trickling sensation as his life's blood ran down his neck and eroded his will to continue the struggle. The action around him unfolded in slow motion; he tried to focus on the scene, tried to force his mind and body to deny his injury.

The remaining agents, now spaced at irregular intervals across the end of the runway, fired repeatedly at the truck. In his deteriorating state Drew thought they looked like a firing squad delivering the ultimate sentencing. The blaze of bullets from every gun converged on the protruding rear of the vehicle.

The Bronco exploded! From the ball of red-orange fury, flames shot skyward, lighting the night with a brilliant flash.

Poetic justice, Drew thought through an encroaching haze of darkness as he watched the angry sphere of fire dwindle to a tiny speck at the end of a long dark tunnel.

Oh, Laine. I love you. "Forgive me," Drew whispered as the ground reached up for him and a soft, silent blackness claimed him.

Chapter 13

"You look like hell," Laine told the reflection in the bathroom mirror. Dark circles rimmed her eyes, her complexion was positively gray and her mouth seemed to have a perpetual droop. Well, why not? Isn't that where she'd been throughout one long night and into another dawn — to hell and back?

"Oh, Drew." She leaned her forehead against the cool glass and sighed. "Where are you? Are you all right?"

The same two questions, plus a thousand more, had plagued Laine throughout the long night past. Sleep was hopeless. Each time she tried, a vivid picture of Drew, pale and weak in a hospital bed, or worse yet, deathly chill and cold, sprang to mind. Laine cautioned herself not to allow such thoughts to take root, but since the conversation with Nelda Patterson, her imagination had been working overtime. There was no solid evidence to support her fear that Drew was involved in the Reese case as anything other than a prosecutor. Until such evidence presented itself, Laine clung to the hope that her fears were groundless.

"Good morning."

Laine thought Donna Marshall's smile was disgustingly bright, but attempted to return it in kind as she entered the jury room. "Good morning, Donna."

The herculean effort Laine had expended at her makeup mirror in order to prepare for her last day of grand jury service seemed to have paid off. Donna didn't comment on the smudges beneath her lower lashes and no one seemed to notice her less-than enthusiastic anticipation for the day's festivities. Laine looked around the room. She was surrounded by smiling faces and gay conversation as Donna, Ruth Jackson, the retired dentist, Dr. Howell, and all the rest sampled the array of goodies brought by the jurors. *They should celebrate. After working hard for eighteen months the group deserved a party.* What they didn't deserve was a wet blanket of a foreman putting a damper on their fun. Resolved at least to pretend to enjoy herself, Laine put on her best smile and joined the conversation.

"Well, guys," said Kathy, the bookstore owner, as she joined the group of jurors clustered at Laine's table, "I never thought we'd see the end of all this fun and games, but it's almost over. I don't know about you, but I've had just about all the fun I can stand."

"So has my boss," Donna replied.

"You know," the ex-cabbie entered the conversation, "I think it was enjoyable and educational." Several jurors turned disbelieving stares on him. "Think about it," he urged. "We've participated in something that is the foundation of modern justice. Without the grand jury system, the innocent in our country might have a much tougher time."

"Yeah? Well, what about the criminals?" came the rebuttal.

"I never said the system was perfect," he replied. "But be honest, didn't you find yourselves looking forward to these sessions? I know I did. And didn't you learn about a lot of laws and stuff you never knew before?"

"Laws and lawbreakers," Donna commented drily.

"Okay, sure. Sometimes the system works for the guilty, but it never works against the innocent. And as long as intelligent citizens can get together in a room, listen to the evidence, then guarantee the accused gets his day in court, we're gonna do fine."

Dr. Howell, who had stood quietly absorbing their comments, spoke up. "I keep remembering all the good we did; the drug dealers we helped take off the streets, the laws we

196

helped to enforce. I think we can be very proud of the last eighteen months. It was time well spent."

"I'll drink to that," Ruth Jackson interjected, lifting a glass of fruit punch supplied by Kathy.

"So will I," chorused Donna and Dr. Howell.

"To the good we've done." The former taxi driver lifted his coffee cup in a toast and they all laughed.

Laine stood at the fringe of the group, still smiling, but continually glancing at the door to the jury room, waiting. At any moment Mr. Elroy would walk through the door and satisfy their curiosity about the results of the previous day's indictment of Donald Barlow and his coconspirators. Would he also satisfy her curiosity about Drew? A knock sounded and Warren Elroy was admitted to the room.

"Good morning, ladies and gentlemen." Wearing a navy business suit and a pleasant smile, he strolled to the prosecutor's table. "Well, if I'd known you were throwing a party, I'd have been here sooner."

"Have some punch," someone said.

"And some cake," another offered.

"Thank you, but I've got a plane to catch shortly and once my sweet tooth tastes cake, we might not be able to lift off." Good-natured laughter floated through the room.

"I understand you're interested in the results of the indictment on the Reese case." Elroy's brows drew together in a frown. Laine's heart jackhammered against her ribcage. "Well . . . we did stop the sale of the laser weapons. And, we did put an end to the traitors. But unfortunately, one agent lost his life and two others were seriously wounded."

Laine's stomach lurched. She bit back a wave of nausea as a sudden premonition of doom settled, shroud-like, around her shoulders.

"A lot of good men worked hard to bring the Reese case

197

to a satisfying conclusion," Elroy continued. "FBI agents, CIA, local law enforcement — all of them combined their efforts on this one. Even the federal prosecutor's office gave this case personal attention. Mr. Kenyon, who first presented the case to the grand jury, was a member of the assault team responsible for apprehending the traitors. Actually, not all the suspects were arrested. Donald Barlow shot our inside man, then was killed when he tried to escape." He paused and took a deep breath. "That's about all I'm certain of at this point. I don't even know the names of the wounded agents."

"Oh dear, what a shame." Ruth Jackson shook her head as Elroy left the room a minute later. "I hope that handsome Mr. Kenyon wasn't the one that got killed."

The lament echoed like a death knell in Laine's heart.

Suddenly, the opposite end of the grand jury room seemed to telescope away from her into a tiny pinpoint, threatening to disappear completely. She couldn't breathe, couldn't move. Her body simply shut itself down and for a moment, Laine thought rather objectively, *I'm going to faint.* But the sensation passed as she gulped a lungful of air. With robotlike movements she placed her glass of punch on the table and groped for the arm of her chair. *Don't panic. Stay calm. You'll be fine if you just don't panic.*

Panic or no, Laine knew she would never be fine again. Not without Drew. *Oh, please God, don't let him be the one. Don't let him be . . .* She couldn't bring herself to complete the thought. *Get hold of yourself. There are people depending on you today. You can't fall apart now.* Eyes closed, one hand firmly covering her mouth, she forced herself to take deep breaths.

"Laine? Laine?"

She glanced at her shoulder and wondered how Donna Marshall's hand had gotten there.

"Hey, Laine, you still with us?"

"What?" She looked up at the secretary as if seeing a total stranger.

"You okay? All of a sudden your color's not so good and you're acting kinda funny."

"Funny," Laine repeated dumbly.

"Laine," Donna's voice became concerned as she saw the stunned expression on the foreman's face. "Look at me. Are you sick? Do you need a doctor?"

"Yes," Laine answered absently, then blinked back to reality. "No. No." She shook her head. "I'm fine. I don't need a doctor."

"You don't look fine."

"Sorry, Donna . . . I guess I let my imagination run away with me. I couldn't help thinking about . . . the . . . agent who was killed."

"Yeah, it's too bad, but at least they got the bad guys, right?"

"Right," Laine whispered, knowing nothing would ever be right again if Drew were dead.

For Laine, the next couple of hours passed in a horrid blur, the only reality occasional spears of agonizing emotional pain to remind her that she was still alive. Each time the pain shot through her, all her willpower was summoned to subdue the hurt and seek the soothing numbness. Functioning on automatic pilot, Laine walked, talked and smiled without knowing what she said or to whom. Her world was falling apart. Nothing mattered — not Palmer's threats or her own misgivings. Only Drew was important. By the time Laine drove into the parking space in front of her building, she was hanging on to her sanity by sheer desperation.

Walking into the cool solitude of her apartment, she dropped her handbag on the table, then stopped at the doorway to her living room. A deafening stillness surrounded her and instinctively she wrapped her arms around her waist, hugging her body protectively. The overwhelming feeling of aloneness detonated flares of searing pain and she fought to subdue her despair. *I must not give up hope. I must not. Drew is alive! He has to be!*

Drew. Her wonderful, loving Drew. If he were . . .

"No!" Laine's vehement refusal ricocheted off the walls of her living room. "No-o-o." The denial became a whispered wail. She wasn't even aware she was crying until the first silent tear splashed onto her bare arm, then another and another. She clenched her jaw to kill the sob of primitive grief rising in her throat. Tears weren't going to help find Drew. And find him she must.

Laine straightened her shoulders, then walked directly to her desk, picked up the telephone and dialed four digits. "Information, I want to speak to your supervisor, please."

In fifteen short minutes, Laine had an alphabetical list of the names and phone numbers of every hospital in the San Antonio area. If she had to move heaven and earth, she would find the man she loved and not even the United States government was going to stop her. Resolutely, she dialed the fifth number on her list.

"Brooks Army Hospital," a drawling female voice announced.

"Yes, do you have a patient by the name of Andrew Kenyon?" Nervously, Laine doodled on the corner of her notepad.

"One moment, please." The operator left the line, then returned a few seconds later. "Registration shows an A. Kenyon having been admitted to emergency around midnight. I'll transfer you."

The pencil in Laine's hand stilled instantly and she gripped it with such force that the pressure snapped the point. Her heart vaulted to a trip-hammer speed. *Please, God, please.*

"Hello." A youthful sounding voice came over the line. "Uh, this is the fourth-floor nurses' station."

"Can —" Laine swallowed hard "— can you tell me Mr. Andrew Kenyon's room number, please."

"Ah, I'm just a candy striper and all the nurses are busy right now. Hang on and I'll see if I can find somebody."

Laine heard the receiver clunk as it met a hard surface, then a swishing noise as though the girl's uniform had brushed against the phone. "Oh!" the same young voice, only fainter, exclaimed to someone at her end. "I was just coming down the hall and the phone rang and everybody was gone and —"

"Problem, Talmage?"

"No ma'am, but there's a lady asking about a Mr. Kenyon. Isn't he the one down at the end of the hall?"

"You didn't mention that to the caller did you, Talmage?"

"No ma'am, I didn't tell her anything, I —"

"All right, but if anyone asks you again, you're not to say anything about the patient at the end of the hall. No information regarding Mr. Kenyon or his condition to anyone, understand?"

"Yes ma'am."

"Good. You're excused. Now hand me the phone and resume your duties."

"This is Captain Griffin, fourth-floor supervisor, may I help you?" The voice was again female but this time much more mature and with definite authority.

Shocked at the conversation she'd overheard, Laine's answer was slow in coming. "I . . . I would like Mr. Kenyon's room number."

"May I ask who told you we had a patient by that name on the fourth floor?"

"The operator transferred me to this extension. She said he came into the emergency room last night around —"

201

"I see. I'm sorry, but you were misinformed."

"What!" Laine couldn't believe her ears.

"I said you have received the wrong information. We have no patient on this floor under that name."

"But I —"

"I'm sorry. We're terribly busy, if you'll excuse me."

"But I have to kn—" The line went dead in Laine's ear.

Stunned, she pulled the receiver away from her cheek and stared at it. Shock rapidly gave way to anger.

What the hell was going on?

Standing, she slammed the receiver back into place, then wound her fingers into tight balls of fury. She had an almost uncontrollable urge to smash the phone into a billion pieces; anything to vent the rage and frustration boiling inside her. In a futile gesture she hit the top of the desk with the side of her clenched fist and wished she hadn't.

"Damn!" She lifted a now-tender knuckle to her mouth. "That does it! Don't get mad, get busy." The tone of her voice held an iron edge. All right, she thought, if they wouldn't give her any information long-distance, she would ask them face to face. And keep on asking until she got the right answer.

Yanking open a drawer, she pulled out a telephone book, flipped pages until she found the section for airlines, then reached for the phone. As her fingertips touched the smooth plastic, the phone shrilled, shattering Laine's nerves. Trembling hands lifted the receiver to her ear.

"Hello."

"Miss Stewart?"

"Yes." She barely recognized her own breathy voice.

"This is Major Cortland, Security, Brooks Army Hospital. I'm calling on behalf of Mr. Kenyon." His voice held the crisp cadence so often identified with the military.

Laine, unable to ask the question that tortured her to the

point of insanity, gripped the edge of the desk. Was Drew alive?

"Miss Stewart?"

"Yes," she whispered, "I'm still here."

"I've been authorized to inform you Mr. Kenyon has been hospitalized and wants to see you."

"Hospitalized? How . . . how badly is he hurt?"

"I'm sorry, but I'm not at liberty to divulge confidential details. I can only say it is imperative you arrive as soon as possible. I only hope you're in time."

Dear God! One still-trembling hand covered her mouth, stifling a gasp.

"A ticket is being held in your name at Texas Airways. Your flight to San Antonio departs at 3:00 P.M. Does that present any time problem for you?"

"No. No, there's no problem," she answered quickly over the choking knot lodged in her throat. "Please, can't you tell me —"

"I will personally meet your flight and transport you directly to Brooks." His statement overrode her question.

"But I need . . . can't you . . ." Her words trailed into silence as her voice broke with emotion.

At the other end of the line the major cleared his throat discreetly. "I hesitate to add to your distress, Miss Stewart, but I caution you not to speak of these arrangements to anyone."

"Of course."

"Then I will await your arrival," he said, and hung up.

Major Cortland had insinuated that Drew's injuries were life threatening. *But at least he's alive.* Her heart almost burst with joy. *He's alive! Drew sent for me . . . he wants to see me. . . .*

As quickly as her joy flowered, it wilted. Major Cortland's words echoed in her head. *"I only hope you're in time."*

She would be in time. She had to be. If determination

counted for anything in this world or the next, Drew would live. Their love was too strong, too beautiful to die. Love beyond reason substantiated her heartfelt conviction, a conviction she clung to desperately as she flung a change of clothes into an overnight bag and dashed to catch her flight.

Once Laine was airborne she was able to calm herself enough to wonder how long the trip from the airport to the hospital would take. How long would they let her see Drew? Stop asking pointless questions, she admonished herself. What difference did any of it make as long as she reached Drew the fastest way possible? In an hour or so she would be with Drew telling him of her love and tomorrow's promise of a wonderful future together. She must hold fast to their dream and not allow doubts or negative questions to deflate her hopes. Drew's injury was cause enough for gloom. Had she come so close to happiness only to have it snatched away? Was losing Drew heaven's price for her all-too-brief visit to paradise?

Laine stepped off the plane a short time later. The San Antonio airport was buzzing with afternoon passengers as she passed the Texas Airways gate and began to search the milling crowd.

"Miss Stewart?" A deep, gravelly voice spoke her name close behind her. Startled, she whirled to face a man of average height, green eyes and uniformed in air-force blue. The nameplate on his coat proclaimed Maj. D. Cortland.

"Major." Her voice carried a tinge of relief. "Thank you for meeting me."

"Glad to be of service. This all of your luggage?" She nodded as he took the overnight bag from her grasp. "If you'll come this way, I have a car waiting."

Without further conversation he led her through the terminal and into the late-afternoon sunshine. The central Texas humidity was suffocating as he assisted her into an unmarked blue sedan. "How was your flight?" he asked politely as they left the airport.

"Fine, thank you. Major —" she began almost immediately, only to have him cut her off with a wave of his hand.

"Miss Stewart, I know you have many questions, and I only wish I could give you answers. However, as I told you on the phone, security regulations must be adhered to. I'm sure Mr. Kenyon will tell you as much as he can when he sees you."

"Then he's not unconscious?"

He cut her a quick glance. "No, where did you hear that? I don't recall giving you such information on the phone."

"You didn't, exactly, but —"

"You haven't spoken to anyone else about Mr. Kenyon, have you? I thought I made it clear strict security must be maintained." His voice had taken on an unpleasant edge she didn't care for.

"No, of course not, but I . . ." Laine sighed wearily. "You must forgive me, Major. I've been so concerned about Drew's — Mr. Kenyon's — condition, my imagination is working overtime."

Laine was relieved to notice his smile was very cordial. "I understand completely, Miss Stewart. Your concern is precisely the reason you're here. Don't worry, I'm sure everything will work out just the way it's supposed to."

She returned a tenuous smile. "I pray you're right, Major Cortland."

"I am," he assured her. "Try to relax. Here, have a piece of candy?" he offered politely, withdrawing a small lusterless foil-wrapped square from his pocket. At a shake of her head, he shrugged and single-handedly unwrapped the candy and shoved it into his mouth.

"How much farther to the hospital?" No matter how hard

Laine tried, relaxing was out of the question.

"We're here."

Laine looked around. She hadn't even noticed they had driven onto the hospital grounds. The imposing brick building loomed just ahead; an intermittent stream of people in uniforms — white, blue and khaki — flowed through the doors and across the campus. Her fingertips touched her lips in a nervous gesture. *Almost there, my love. Hold on. I'm coming.*

A minute later, Major Cortland's hand lightly grasped her arm just above the elbow as he assisted her from the car and guided her toward the emergency entrance. At the massive double doors he whisked off his hat, tucking it securely under his left arm as he opened the door for Laine. Once inside, his left hand returned to her elbow. They walked through the spacious lobby, then down a wide hall until they reached a bank of elevators. While inside the elevator, he released her arm, only to reestablish his hold the minute the doors opened before they stepped into the fourth-floor hallway.

Laine was on the verge of questioning his solicitude when the major's fingers intensified the pressure on her arm. Fighting the unexplainable urge to jerk free, she glanced up to see two airmen walking toward them, engrossed in animated conversation. Straightening to a brisk walk when they caught sight of Major Cortland, the pair snapped a crisp salute, their fingertips touching their foreheads precisely as they passed Laine and her guide.

Laine frowned when she noticed the rather off-handed return as Cortland's hand performed a weak imitation of the airmen's gesture. The pressure on Laine's arm had increased to the point of causing pain. Instinctively, she started to pull away.

"Here we are." The unexpected coldness in his voice stilled her efforts and she jerked her head up quickly.

The number on the door read 408. Suddenly, Laine's whole body began to tremble. On the other side of the door was the man she loved, wounded, perhaps fatally. But he mustn't see fear in her eyes — only love, all her love. She stiffened her spine and gave herself a mental shake as she reached out, clutched the handle on the door and gave it a firm push.

He stood at the window, his back to the door. Laine's heart hammered so loudly, she half expected Drew to turn at the noise. But he stood very still, his head bent.

Thank God, he's all right! At least he looked all right. Dressed in slacks and a sports shirt, he didn't appear wounded at all.

"Drew." His name was the faintest of whispers.

Drew jerked his head up abruptly, his whole body rigid as he listened. For a split second he believed . . . His shoulders slumped. *You imagined she called your name, didn't you? You're in worse shape than you thought, Kenyon. Laine doesn't even know where you are and if she did, they wouldn't let her see you.* His right hand raked through his hair at the same moment he turned toward the bed, wincing as the movement unintentionally tugged the bandage on his forehead. Instantly pain ceased to exist, as did everything else save the single point of reference that now filled his vision, mind and heart.

Laine standing beside . . .

Laine moved forward, intending to rush into Drew's arms the instant he saw her. But her body was abruptly and violently jerked backward, slamming her roughly against the major's rock-hard body.

Eyes widened in shock, her gaze met Drew's across the sterile silence of the room. His face was not lit in a smile of welcome, but was carved into hard lines of loathing. He spoke not to her, but to the man who restrained her.

"Take your hands off her, Barlow!"

Drew's icy command cracked the quiet room like a cannon shot at the exact instant Laine felt a cold hard object touch the throbbing pulse at her right temple.

Chapter 14

"Been a long time, Kenyon."

"Let her go."

"When it suits me."

Drew stepped forward and the unmistakable click of a pistol's hammer being drawn back reverberated through the room. Drew froze. "She has nothing to do with any of this."

"That's where you're wrong, ole buddy; she had everything to do with it. This —" Barlow gave Laine's arm a swift yank "— delightful creature, is my ticket out of here."

The musky odor of gun oil momentarily obliterated the antiseptic smell of the hospital room, asaulting Laine's nostrils to the point of nausea. Her stomach alternately lurched, then twisted itself into a hard knot as undisguised fear quickly replaced shock. Her gaze shot to Drew.

He was granite, finely chiseled and implacable, cold except for the rage and murderous intent firing the depths of his blue eyes.

Unrelenting terror stalked every corner of her mind as the inevitability of death became a tangible presence, a taste in her mouth, a chill against her skin. One of them, maybe all of them, would soon be dead.

"You won't get away with this."

"Watch me." Barlow's voice was steady, soft.

"I should have killed you when I had the chance back in Nam."

"Never did say thank-you for your generosity, Kenyon. Lucky for me you have a conscience."

"Obviously, you suffer no such deterrent."

"I don't suffer, period. But you will."

"By your hand?" Drew shook his head slowly. "Not the longest day you live, which, if I have my wish, is today."

Barlow grinned. "Still the same old Kenyon, out to rid the world of all its rotten apples. Too bad you proved to be mortal like the rest of us." A deliberate jerk caused Laine to wince and Drew to stiffen.

"If you hurt her, you'll never leave this room alive."

"Drew —"

"Shut up!" Barlow ground out of the side of his mouth, cutting off Laine's whispered plea. At the sound of her voice, Barlow's control slipped precariously. His chest heaved, his eyes narrowed and his mouth went slack. The business end of the revolver quivered against Laine's temple and a tear crowded the corner of her eye.

A low guttural sound came from Drew.

"That's it, Kenyon. Come on, play hero. You're so good at it."

The taunt struck its mark and for a horrifying moment, Laine felt certain Drew was doomed. Barlow's anger was an electric presence beside her, his rage bouncing off her like sparks off a downed power line.

"What do you want in exchange for Miss Stewart?"

"Miss Stewart? So formal, Kenyon. You weren't so righteous in that Dallas parking lot, or in Cancún. Bet you called her other things besides Miss Stewart. What erotic words you must have whispered in her ear! Huh, Kenyon?"

Laine's spinning, fragmented thoughts stilled and fell into place. Barlow was baiting Drew! He wanted Drew to come for him so he could shoot Drew down in cold blood.

Hands knotted into tight fists, Drew sought and found the constraint required if he and Laine were to stay alive.

"You didn't concoct this elaborate ruse just to put a bullet through my brain. Before the smoke cleared, you'd have every hospital employee on this floor crashing through the door in seconds. You're not stupid, Barlow. What do you want?" Drew's voice was deadly calm.

Eyes cut sharply to the right, Laine watched their adversary. Barlow licked fat, dry lips and swallowed hard. A half grin, half sneer crooked his mouth.

"A compliment? I'm touched." The smirk vanished. "Simply put, I want you, Kenyon. The minute after the truck hit the dirt, so did I. I knew by the time the bureaucrats were able to form another capture plan I could resurrect myself and get to you. I can't tell how relieved I was to hear from my highly reliable sources you were still alive. All the time I was crawling away from those brainless agents I prayed I hadn't been robbed of the pleasure of killing you. It didn't matter what I had to go through so long as I could see you dead. Now, you might say I'll be killing two birds with one stone."

"Name your terms."

"No terms. I told you pure and simple. There's a small private jet waiting for me at a nearby airport. After I finish with you and your lady, I fly off into the sunset." He was relishing every moment that Drew was at his mercy. "I have a car outside and you're going to be my chauffeur. Sort of like driving yourself to your own funeral. And don't even think about trying any funny stuff or your lady's beautiful head's gonna have a big hole in it." Another pause. "Do we understand each other, Kenyon?"

"Perfectly."

"Good."

"What happens when we reach the plane?"

"Your lady and I are goin' on a little trip."

"Where to?"

"Not thirty seconds ago you said I wasn't stupid. So don't

play games with me, Kenyon. You've got too much to lose."

"What about Laine?"

"Oh, don't worry, I'll take good care of her. As soon as we land in a country without an extradition treaty, she'll be as free as a bird."

"What guarantee do I have of her safety?"

"Only my word."

"Which we both know is worthless."

"Careful, Kenyon, you don't wanna call my hand."

Drew paused, admitting the truth of the boast to himself. "What choice do I have? You hold all the aces."

"Exactly. Now —" Barlow stepped to one side, taking Laine with him "— the three of us are going for a stroll, down the hall and out the emergency entrance. If anyone stops us or asks any questions on the way, remember how much value you place on your lady's life. No sudden moves when you open the door. Check the hallway, then stay directly in front of us. Once outside the hospital, I'll direct you to the car."

"And you —" without glancing her way, he released Laine's right arm and in the same swift movement resecured his hold by clamping his left arm around her waist "—pretend we are a loving couple visiting a friend. And make it look good. Your life and his depend on it. Don't attempt any sly glances to attract attention. Got it?"

Laine gave an infinitesimal nod of her head. The pistol followed the motion.

"Move, Kenyon."

Slowly, Drew moved forward. His gaze never left Laine's face. Wordlessly she pleaded with him not to act upon the blood lust she saw in his eyes. Silently she begged, *Please, Drew, don't! He'll kill you!*

Drew tore his gaze from Laine's pleading look and walked to the door. Barlow swung Laine to face Drew's broad back.

An indrawn breath answered the hard thrust of the pistol against her temple . . . then the pressure disappeared.

"Listen carefully, Kenyon. Our public appearance doesn't lessen my threat one iota. The gun's in my pocket and my finger's on the trigger. If you so much as glance my way, or stump your toe, she'll be dead. Open the door. Remember: no sudden moves."

The trio moved inconspicuously into the hospital corridor.

Each step Laine took sent a tremor through legs threatening to give way. She didn't noticed her surroundings; her attention remained trained on Drew's back. Mesmerized, she watched his shoulders ripple beneath his blue shirt. With each step, his neck cords tightened, his fists clenched. An awesome sense of leashed power exuded from the tightly wound body of the man she loved. The power surrounded her, embuing her with a renewed feeling of hope. She could not lose control of her emotions now, she cautioned herself as they stepped from the elevator on the ground floor. How much longer could the terrible nightmare last?

"Hold it."

Barlow's low command brought the threesome to a halt before the main emergency-room entrance. "The doors operate electronically, but don't get any funny ideas. We'll all go through at the same time. Ready . . . go!"

The automatic doors whirred open to admit the sound of a wailing siren just as they stepped through.

The heat of the Texas summer evening hit the trio like a furnace blast. The siren noise increased, funneling into the concrete breezeway. Glancing left, Laine noted the area was virtually deserted except for a scruffy-looking construction worker assisting an equally ragged man who hobbled toward the emergency entrance. Several cars were parked to her right, away from the main entrance, all empty.

Laine's hopes for help sank.

By now, the scream of the siren was ear-splitting as its source came careening into view. Slanted at a dangerous angle, two wheels barely touching the ground, an ambulance rounded the corner, swerved into the driveway and came to a screeching halt directly in front of the escapees. A second identical vehicle pulled in behind the first. Twin domes flashed glaring red lights and dual sirens wound to a slow moan, then faded away. Even before the vehicles came to a full stop, the doors flew open to pour forth men and equipment.

Drew, Laine and Barlow were momentarily stunned into immobility as the previously quiet area was transformed into bedlam.

Paramedics yelled instructions while hauling body-laden gurneys through the gaping ambulance doors. White-coated hospital employees gushed from the building to assist. In the blink of an eye the area leading up to the emergency entrance had swelled from five people to what looked like five hundred. Orders were shouted, equipment clanked and rattled, doors slammed on a continuing stream of arriving cars and everyone moved at once. The noise level became deafening . . . and distracting.

Stupefied, Laine blinked; to her left, two paramedics rushed past with a victim-laden stretcher.

"Damn!" Exasperation and anger permeated Barlow's voice. "Kenyon!" he yelled. "Kenyon, move out to the right!" Barlow's urgent command was lost in the racket. Drew did not move. "Damn!" Two steps propelled Barlow forward. At that precise moment Drew darted to the right and Barlow found himself directly in the path of a rapidly oncoming gurney.

"What the hell —" Barlow tried to sidestep the narrow, sheet-covered projectile. His instinctive reaction widened the gap between his body and Laine's from one inch to more than a foot. Barlow's grasp on her arm slipped. With a desperate jerk Laine found her freedom. Barlow quickly lunged for Laine, but not quickly enough.

The occupied stretcher hurled forward, striking Barlow squarely in the solar plexus, pinning his gun hand to his side. A grunt whooshed from Barlow and he bent at the waist.

The "victim" rolled off the gurney, positioning himself between the two paramedics. Precipitously, every "paramedic," every "victim," every "hospital employee" turned their attention . . . and their guns on Barlow.

Unseen arms unexpectedly grabbed Laine's torso and she felt herself falling. The body attached to the arms broke her fall, then shielded her. Cheek pressed against the hot cement, she was trapped, unable to see. But she could hear . . .

"Kenyon!"

Barlow's death-knell scream ripped into Laine's heart.

A shot rang out.

Then the sound of scrambling feet and gunfire seemed to come from every direction at once. She struggled for freedom, but the body covering hers would not budge. The retort of guns and pings of bullets grazing concrete seemed interminable as Laine strained to catch the sound of Drew's voice among the hoarse shouts. She did not hear him.

The shooting ceased. A ringing silence prevailed.

Her "bodyguard" relinquished his post and Laine struggled for a deep breath of air. She pushed herself up on one cement-scraped elbow. A giant hand appeared before her eyes and she looked up into the smiling face of a burly, white-smocked man.

"Sorry to be so rough, Miss Stewart. Let me help you up?" Bewildered, she trustingly placed her hand in his and a second later found herself staring at his shirt collar. Before she could speak, he stepped aside, giving her a full view of the emergency area. A gasp rocketed into her throat, both hands clamped over her mouth. The giant hand again steadied her.

Donald Barlow lay sprawled, faceup, blood pulsing from multiple wounds.

Laine's stomach rebelled and she turned away. Eyes wide with fear, her head snapped up to face the man beside her. He read the question in her tear-filled gaze and turned his head away.

"Hey, somebody needs to take care of this lady."

"I believe that job belongs to me."

Laine spun around, almost losing her balance. Familiar, strong, loving arms enfolded her.

The Cancún sun had only begun to herald the day when Laine opened her eyes.

"Good morning."

She snuggled closer, her head automatically seeking a favorite spot on her husband's chest — her ear directly over his heart. "Hmm."

"It looks like a perfect day outside."

"Hmm."

"What do you want to do with your perfect day?" He kissed a cluster of velvet curls on her forehead.

"Hmm-m-m-m." Her answer was a cross between a soft growl and a purr.

"Yeah, me too. And after that?"

"As a matter of fact," she murmured, loving the sleep-warm scent of him, "there is something I want to do."

"Name it."

"Talk."

"Talk?"

"Yes. Talk to me, Drew." Her voice held a note of concern.

"I thought I'd answered all your questions."

Gently, she pushed away and scooted upward in the bed

216

until they were at eye level. "In the three days since we married, you've told me —"

"That I love you at least a million times." He smiled.

"Yes. And about John Rankin." She knitted her brow as she itemized all Drew had revealed. "And some unbelievable shoot-out in San Antonio and your superficial wound." She kissed a spot on his forehead just below the small bandage. "You've talked about being the bait to draw Barlow out into the open, and —"

"Your fabulously soft derriere."

"Drew." She tried to look exasperated but failed. "We talked about how Barlow must have been watching you for months and saw us together, probably followed us to Cancún. How Rankin had your hospital room bugged and had to improvise when Barlow showed up with me in tow. You told me —"

"I can't get enough of you, of the way you make love to me."

"Ah . . . you, ah . . . you've told me all the paramedics and victims were Rankin's men in disguise, and how there was a hidden microphone in your hospital room, but . . ."

"But?"

"You haven't told me the one thing I want to hear."

"Only one?"

"Will you *promise* me no more playing secret agent."

"I was never a *secret* agent. Lots of people knew."

"Drew, be serious! I thought I'd lost you. Not once, but twice. I couldn't go through that kind of agony again."

All teasing stopped and he quickly gathered her into his arms. "Neither could I. When I saw you standing beside Barlow, his gun at your head, I died a thousand deaths. None of them torturous enough in comparison to the anguish I saw in your eyes. For the first time in my life I experienced the paralyzing fear of losing someone I loved. I don't *ever* want

217

another similar experience."

"Drew?"

"Set your mind at rest, my lovely Laine." His thumb stroked her cheek. "From now on I'm just a plain ole lawyer."

"A married lawyer," she amended.

"Definitely. Now, you tell me what *I* want to hear."

"I love you. Now, forever, always."

"Sweet-talker," he murmured as his mouth took hers in a soul-binding, bone-melting kiss.

About the Author

Sandy Steen spent many an hour daydreaming while growing up in the Texas Panhandle. Later, inspired by her husband of more than twenty years and her two children, Sandy decided to put her dreams on paper.

Although her family had some doubts when they first observed her methods of staring into space for endless hours while she plotted her stories, they are her staunchest supporters. Sandy herself believes that if she can make a reader believe in the wonder of fantasy and feel the joy of falling in love, then she has indeed succeeded.